Lassitude and other stories

CONTEMPORARY PHILIPPINE FICTION

# Lassitude

## and other stories

# Cárlos Cortés

—— Anvil ——

*Lassitude and other stories*
*Cárlos Cortés*

Published and exclusively distributed by
ANVIL PUBLISHING, INC.
2/F Team Pacific Building
13 Jose Cruz Streets
1604 Pasig City
Philippines
Telephones: 671.1888, 671.9230 (publishing dept.);
671.1899 (sales & marketing dept.)
Fax: 914.0155
Email: anvil@fc.emc.com.ph

The National Library of the Philippines CIP Data

Recommended entry:

Cortés, Cárlos
    Lassitude and other stories
/ Cárlos Cortés - Pasig City :
Anvil Pub., c1998
    1 v

    1. Short stories, Philippine (English).
I. Title.

PL5546   899.21'03   1998   P981000004
ISBN 971-27-0691-5


Cover art by ANTONIO B. CORTÉS
        ("Dog in the Manger," watercolor, 1978)
Cover design by ALBERT BORRERO
Interior design by GERRY BACLAGON of Word House

Printed in the Philippines
by Cacho Hermanos, Inc.

for my mother, Josefina B. Cortés (1927-1995)

# acknowledgments

• cover: "Dog in the Manger," watercolor by Antonio B. Cortés, copyright © 1978.

• In "Thirteen Ways...": lyrics from "Tin Man" by the America (words & music by Dewey Bunnell, copyright © 1978, Warner Bros. Music Corp) and paraphrased lyrics from "Money for Nothing" by Dire Straits (words & music by Mark Knopfler & Gordon Matthew Sumner, copyright © 1989, Virgin Music).

• In "Close to the Bone": lyrics from "Honky-Tonk Women" by the Rolling Stones (words & music by Mick Jagger & Keith Richard, copyright © 1971, Decca Records) and from "I Still Haven't Found What I'm Looking For" by U2 (words & music by J. Bono & U2, copyright © 1986, Island Records).

• In "Du-awon" the italicized fragment about sirens and moonlight is from the "Free Fall" chapter of Eric Gamalinda's novel *The Empire of Memory* (Manila, 1992).

• "Thirteen Ways..." takes its structure from Wallace Stevens's famous poem and John L'Hereux's 1978 *Atlantic Monthly* story "Thirteen Ways of Looking at a Blackbird or, The Priest's Wife", its physics theories from Stephen W. Hawking's *A Brief History of Time* (London, 1990), and much of its space trivia from *Lift-Off* by Michael Collins (Washington D.C., 1988).

• "Close to the Bone" owes most of its facts and knowledge to Ramon Echevarria's *Rediscovery in Southern Cebu* (Cebu City, 1974).

- "Glossolalia" borrows its title and meter from John Barth's examples in *Lost in the Funhouse* (New York, 1974).

- "Kukri" owes most of its facts and knowledge to Edward Bishop's *Better to Die: The Story of the Gurkhas* (London, 1976)

- "Fatal Augury" borrows from Rafael Palma's *Biografía de Rizal* (OFICINA DE BIBLIOTECAS PÚBLICAS, Manila, 1949); from "Caviteño Kitchen" by Gilda Cordero-Fernando, "The Capture of Aguinaldo" by Carlos Quirino, and "Guerrilla in Samar" by Jovenal Velasco, all three articles from Volume 8 of *Filipino Heritage: The Making of a Nation* (Lahing Pilipino Publishing, Inc., Manila, 1978); from "Balangiga Story: Massacre or Victory?" by Charo Nabong-Cabardo in the September 24, 1995 SUNSTAR WeekEnd Magazine; from *Tabunan: the Untold Exploits of the Famed Cebu Guerrillas in World War II* by Manuel F. Segura (Cebu City, 1975); and from *De Mi Pluma* by José M. Basa, (Manila, 1939, reissued Cebu City, 1981). The translation of "A Una Bayadera" is by Josefina B. Cortés and the genealogy of the Basas courtesy of José Basa Lugay.

- First publications: "Vietnik" in METRO, December 1993; "Who Loves to Lie With Me" in TAIPAN, May 1995; "Close to the Bone" in METRO, October 1995; "Enosis" and "Glossolalia" in THE EVENING PAPER, August 25-28, 1996; "Stonehenge" in the FREE PRESS, April 12, 1997; and "Kukri" in the GRAPHIC. June 30, 1997. A vignette from "Fatal Augury" appeared in *Caracoa 27* (December 1996).

# contents

Enosis.........................................................1

Vietnik ......................................................3

Black Hole ................................................15

Close to the Bone ....................................53

Du-Awon d/w Notes from Underwater.......................67

Who Loves to Lie With Me ......................93

Kukri ......................................................101

Glossolalia ..............................................117

Stonehenge ............................................119

James, the Brother of Jesus .....................137

Cadibarrawirracanna ..............................145

Fatal Augury ..........................................157

# Enosis

My conception was normal: Y-chromosomed sperm cell from my father's loins, the winner of the tadpole swimming contest, uniting with X-chromosomed egg cell in my mother's uterus. Mitosis ensued, and here atypical things began to happen. The zygote's first division produced two new zygotes, and now we were identical twins in the womb. We might have become Siamese twins had not one embryo atrophied and somehow become absorbed by the other. The surviving fetus developed normally, came to term, and emerged as a baby boy.

I was two years old when the eggsized lump in my peritoneal cavity was diagnosed as a benign tumor. The specialists recommended its surgical removal. My mother took me to an old rural physician, the doctor who had delivered her. He felt and squeezed my lump with his fingers. "This is your twin brother," he told me, although I was too young to understand such words.

My parents arranged for an operation at the city's best hospital. My grandfather, my father's father, hugged me and told me the spirits wanted me back. He would not let them, he whispered.

Three days before the scheduled operation, my grand-father suddenly died. The village midwife said it was his way of cancelling the debt to the spirits. There would be no need for surgery now. The old country doctor, who was the only one my mother really trusted, concurred. Sixty years of practice had given him a keen sense for the mysteries of the human body.

Against the opinion of the city doctors, my parents called off the operation.

The tumor was gone in a couple of weeks, leaving me no memory of it. My mother told me the story when I became old enough to understand words like "tumor" or "cancel." Like a child, I believed it all. As a young adult, I grew to be skeptical of the tale, due to its utter lack of scientific plausibility and factual documentation. But if mitosis meant so much when I was a single cell, now it is enosis that matters, ενοσισ, union, oneness, things cohering (or becoming coherent), falling into place... so that today, on the whole, I think it must have been all true, precisely because of that lack.

# Vietnik

Eemee, our village idiot, loved to party. He could smell a feast a mile off and had the knack for showing up, barefoot and in raggedy short pants, at the most embarrassing moments. The day the mayor's daughter got married, Eemee crashed the reception at His Honor's big house. How had he gotten in? No one knew. It must have been while we were all engrossed in watching the bride maneuver her long satin train out of the beribboned, flower-bedecked white Mercedes-Benz. Flashbulbs were popping, skyrockets whooshing up, and there he was, right in the center of the courtyard, Eemee again. Surrounded by guys ribbing him. This was Mandaue after all, the small town to the north of Cebu City, a place famed for such delicacies as *bibingka* and *tagaktak*, a place where everyone knew everyone.

Eemee was now bedazzling the crowd with his antics. The groom, scion of a wealthy Chinese *mestizo* family from the city, wasn't sure if this was supposed to be the surprise number in the program. The bride, who had never looked more beautiful, was too well-bred to show her discomfiture. She kept on smiling sweetly, as if this sort of thing always happened at wedding receptions. Eemee had a lighted cigarette in his mouth and was working it, with only tongue and teeth, until he got it inverted: filter end poking out, lit end inside his mouth. Then he puffed a few times, cheeks ballooned, showily exhaling smoke through flared nostrils. The crowd loved it. Eemee was squinting, his eyes smarting from the smoke, but still he kept his hands away from the cigarette. Then, wall-eyed face going into contortions as he worked teeth and tongue, he got it flipped over again and there it was, still glowing. He took it by thumb and index finger and delicately tapped off the ash. By this time the mayor had signalled to an aide, who hustled Eemee out of sight to the dirty kitchen in back. There he could eat his fill. The guys in the drinking circle there passed him the glass. Eemee gagged on the imported Scotch whiskey, so they mollified him with a slice of wedding cake.

Eemee got around quite a lot back then, in the sixties. He set a kind of standard: a soirée did not become a real shebang until Eemee showed up to grace it with his presence. There were those who drove him away unfed, people who didn't know better. They always found out it was bad luck to do that; something or other invariably went wrong at their parties.

In the seventies I saw less of Eemee, not that I was keeping track of him. My interests were broadening, and Mandaue was booming. By the eighties it had become a big city. In the mid-eighties I migrated a few miles east, to Mactan Island. By the end of the decade Mandaue had officially become a highly urbanized city with an annual income of 53 million pesos and a population of 180,283. I guessed these estimates to be conservative. The real figures, the way I could feel them in my gut, were probably twice or thrice those. Mandaue was filling up with strangers. I could no longer recognize the passersby when I hung out at my parent's house. Fields where I used to suck stolen sugarcane were sprouting huts and shanties. Bamboo groves had stopped swaying and solidified into highrises. Land that used to sell for a few centavos a square meter now went for several thousand pesos per.

What I couldn't understand was how everything could grow big faster than I could. The Mandaue of my earliest memories was not too different from the small town my father knew, yet my nephews and nieces (for my own children will no longer call it home) seem fated to think of it as a dusty metropolis where gridlock chokes them up every time a brownout kills the traffic lights.

In the sixties Mandaue was much more genteel, or, if you like, backward and provincial. As a little boy, I could climb any tree I fancied. It didn't matter whose backyard it was. They all knew my father, although he was nobody special, just another neighbor. In those days Mandaue, before it became a chartered city, was a "municipality." That must have sounded better than calling it a "town." On the other hand, Cebu City was "the city" and we always called it simply that, as if mentioning its proper name were superfluous. (Calling it "Sugbu" as the old folk did was considered unchic, while the single word "Cebu" meant the whole island.)

These were words we took up in school. None of my teachers ever acknowledged the truth of the matter, that in fact Mandaue was virtually a mere suburb of The City. True, it had its own mayor and was too far away to be annexed; it was what might be termed today an exurb. All I knew was that it lacked everything. Nothing could be done but that you had to go to the city for it. I even had to be born in the city. Things had changed in one generation; expectant parents no longer called for the village *manghihilot* to act as midwife, and so I could not be born in my father's house the way he had been born in his father's house. Came my time to enter this world, my parents had to hail a taxi and rush to a hospital in the city.

School, too, meant Cebu City. Shopping, seeing a movie, dining in a good restaurant—all of these meant going to the city. We might as well have moved to the city and saved ourselves all that commuting. But my father's land was in Mandaue. His family had been in Mandaue since pre-Hispanic times, and it was unthinkable for him to live, or die, anywhere else.

Growth accelerated after the mayor decided to keep Mandaue's business taxes lower than the city's. The San Miguel Corporation established a brewery and a glass plant in Mandaue, and that set the trend. The Lahug Airport at the city's outskirts was closed down and commercial air traffic moved across to Mactan Island and the fine runway the US Air Force had built there. Mandaue, smack between the city and the offshore islet, was caught in the middle. Its growth rate became, for a time, the highest in the country.

By now, old enough to read the newspapers, I had become an avid space buff. I worshipped the astronauts and hung on their every word. "All systems GO," I'd say, whenever my uncles and their smart new wives asked me, at family gatherings, how I was. I also read the stories on the Indochina conflict. The US President was escalating involvement there even as he underwent a gallbladder operation. Later, at his Texas ranch, Johnson lifted his shirt to show the press the incision, a long gash down the convoluted topography of his paunch. A cartoonist made a classic out of it: LBJ lifts his shirt, points to the flesh thus exposed. Even with all the bandages, the scar is clearly a map of Vietnam.

At the Mactan Airport, my father's business trips were less and less on propeller aircraft and more and more on the new jets. Once, taking a midnight flight because of its cheaper "Mercury" fare, he led us, my mother and I, to the viewing deck for a few minutes before he boarded. He pointed to the far end of the runway. There, he told me, on the apron connecting the far ends of the runway and the taxiway, look sharp now. Then I saw them: two huge B-52s, dwarfed by distance, blended into the night, momentarily exposed by the headlights of the gas truck. Mactan was just the right distance for a refuelling stop between Guam and Vietnam.

Some of my neighbors, fresh entrants to the job market, began looking for work in Mactan rather than in the city. One of them reported seeing Eemee over there, hanging around with the workers at the airbase. The USAF servicemen got a kick out of the cigarette stunt. It seemed to work even better with blue-seal cigarettes. They'd give Eemee some free chow every now and then, and the poor fool, always eager, would do odd jobs for them, manual labor, nothing hazardous, loading bombs on their B-52s or something—probably the first time Eemee had ever done real work. He must have found those Americans good company. They were cool guys, down-home farmboys or "Aw, shucks" yokels, ethnic Italians, blacks, Jews, Poles and Chicanos, a pretty tolerant bunch, no nasty rednecks. They'd ask Eemee to choose between seven Lincoln pennies and a single Roosevelt dime. Eemee invariably took the handful of cents. They'd laugh, but it didn't matter all that much, the way we saw it. The moneychangers didn't care for coins, either. They only took greenbacks.

In Mandaue we razzed Eemee another way. We'd ask him about the time he undressed a woman. He got as far as her panties, then took those off, too. And then? Well, he tore off the garter, so he could make a slingshot with it.

Mandaue became a chartered city at the end of the sixties, but even in the early seventies we still had to go to the city to catch a movie or dine in a fancy place. The mayor would not allow moviehouses in Mandaue. He felt movie sex and violence would cause a deterioration of Mandaue's moral standards. I didn't buy that view, because anyone could go to the city and see all those movies there. But of course my opinion didn't count. It was years before I could vote. Besides, the Catholic Women's League, the Jaycees, the Rotary Club, the Kiwanis Club, the Mandaue Lions and the Knights of Columbus were all solidly behind the mayor on this issue. So, no movie theaters, no motels, no fine restaurants. It was obvious that a city without the first two didn't need the third.

For all that, Mandaue was proud of its mayor. Once, a town in the north asked if they could borrow him for a term or two. Perhaps their roads would get paved then. After his triple bypass operation in the United States, the mayor expressed a desire to step down. Mandaue wouldn't hear of it. There really was nobody else in those years. None of his political opponents looked remotely capable of unseating him in the forthcoming elections. I didn't even know who his predecessor had been. I knew his father had been mayor himself, in *his* time, but no one could recall who had kept the seat warm in the interval.

When the President, still in his first term, announced that the country would send a contingent to Vietnam, my father snorted. Marcos, he said, was a puppet of the Americans. To emphasize its noncombat functions the contingent was called the Philippine Civic Action Group, or the PHILCAG. My father called it the PHILCAGeron, working in the Visayan word for "mangy dog." The first batch included an Army engineer from Mandaue. The day he left for Manila en route to Da Nang the whole town sent him off in a motorcade, sirens wailing all the way to the Mactan Airbase. This was before the Bridge had been built. Crossing the Mactan Channel, our vehicles filled up the big barge. Mandaue was going to war, but in a modern, humanitarian way. Our engineer would not bloody his hands. American napalm would do the dirty work.

Down in Mandaue I did my thing, but kept it simple. I toured my hometown on my first bicycle. I went past the borders and saw Consolacion, Banilad, and Lahug. This was my world, and a whole wide world it was. Nothing much happened in it. Things happened only in the papers. Men from earth were going to the moon. Before the decade was out, as JFK had promised. Elsewhere, people were tripping on angst. In Paris, students were out on the streets protesting—what, I never really figured out. In San Francisco, too, they were demonstrating. Make love, they chanted, not war. In London, John Lennon returned his MBE.

It was all so far away. Most of the time it seemed unreal. Still, we were picking up the patois and the counterculture as we took to wearing bellbottom jeans, tie-dyes, and shoulderlength hair. Everyone sported beads, loved flower power, gave peace a chance, turned on to Jesus or became a yogi, and said, "Wow, man, that's groovy, I dig it."

A cousin of mine, Monching el tisoy, a bearded UP undergrad, came over for the summer. One of the girls (it must have been Odette or Arlynne) learned his birthday was on the morrow. We plotted a surprise party. At the appointed hour we sprang up with placards:

"Happy bourgeois birthday, male chauvinist pig!"

or

"Down with imperialism and birthdays!"

or some such thing.

The best piece came last: a papier-mâché figure of the celebrant, hanged by the neck, eyes popping out, tongue swollen. Thus did we burn him in effigy. Then we sat down around a bonfire and roasted wieners and marshmallows on bamboo sticks. We had a cooler of beer and two guitars, and we sang rock ballads and folk songs far into the night.

On my third bottle I noticed that one of the girls, the one named Arlynne, had her eye on me. She was my elder by two years, an impossible gap. Jing Mercado, who was alternating with me on one of the guitars, pointed her out.

"That one's got the hots for you, man," he whispered. "Bet she wouldn't mind if you made a slingshot with her garters."

"If she's so hot," I retorted, "why don't you go after her?"

"Look who's talking! Why me, of all people? Doesn't he know it's him she's got eyes for? Can't he see that?"

It was his shift to the third person that convinced me. In Visayan, that's done for emphasis.

And so I went, in my fumbling way, after her. One afternoon during the siesta hour, on a fallen log shaded by gumamela bushes in their yard, I was just getting to second base when one of the guys called out.

"Hey, come on! Everybody!"

With that we piled, hastily buttoning up, into Ben Yeh's Jeep. Another motorcade, Jude Mayol said. On the way to the Ouano Landing, two more of the gang, Bador Ngoho and James Dean Otikits, flagged us down, ran alongside, clambered aboard and squeezed in. The mayor, Judy Boy repeated, had received a telegram. From some general. No, not RP, but a goddamn USAF general. It notified him of the arrival aboard MATS aircraft of someone from Da Nang. ETA Mactan AFB 1600H.

"What kind of plane?" Arlynne asked.

"MATS," Judy Boy said. "Military Air Transport System."

"Who's the VIP?" I queried.

"We don't know yet," Ben Yeh said.

"Probably PHILCAG," Judy Boy said.

"No," Bador Ngoho said, "Vietcong." His harelip made it sound like "Nyet-tung."

"Right on, man," James Dean Otikits said, "some of those Vietcong look like they're from Mandaue, too."

"Could be a beatnik," Arlynne said.

"Vietnik," Jing Mercado said.

We sped down the Pusok highway, our sirens and mo- torcycle escorts bullying all other traffic off to the road shoulders. Past the airline terminals, we drew up at the airbase gate. American MPs spoke briefly with the mayor in the lead car, examined a piece of paper, then let us all in. A camouflaged Lockheed C-130 Hercules flew low overhead. "Hey, man, psychedelic!" Bador Ngoho said. A black master sergeant escorted the mayor to the edge of the field. The brass band from the Nuestra Señora de Lourdes Barrio Association fell into formation.

And then the Lockheed had touched down and growled to a stop at the far end of the runway. Only its tail could be seen in the distance as it turned into the taxiway. We were aware of the mayor's men running and rolling out a red carpet they had borrowed from the tall, balding American quartermaster, but we could not take our eyes off the C-130, now growing bigger and noisier as it drew near. We all plugged our ears with our index fingers. The ramp marshall, Mickey Mouse headphones on, waved the Herc in with his paddles. The low, squat, warpaint-mottled aircraft, taxiing in on the inner two of its four propellers, seemed to have been lent by its highwing configuration a kind of menacing beauty. It braked to a stop just where the red carpet indicated, its two props somehow reversing spin before they froze.

*Chocks on*, signalled the ramp marshall, tips of paddles touching together. The rear ventral door was lowered. The band struck up a resounding tune. The man from Vietnam emerged, blinking as his eyes met the harsh glare of the summer sun. It was Eemee.

The command pilot chatted briefly with the mayor.

"Shoulda seen this fella come outta that ole B-52 back there," he said, poking his thumb in a westerly direction. "Danged if he don't stir up quite a fuss. Two seconds flat, and they got him surrounded by M-16s. But he's real cool, gotta hand him that. Didn' say a whole lotta nuthin'. Jes' bums a cig'rette off'n the CO and smokes it lit end in his mouth, y'know? The gen'ral couldn't git nuthin' outta him neither, 'cept that he doan' come from Mack Tan at all. He from Mand Howie. That yore place, ain't it?"

"What about you, where are you from?"

"Me? Oh, I'm from Oklahoma."

"Well, I couldn't place your accent."

"Yeah, same problem they had with him."


There was nothing for it but to put Eemee into one of the cars and take him home. The mayor managed to keep it out of the papers, although we rather expected he would have a hard time living it down. Certainly his political opponents must have thought so. They had to suppress their smirks whenever they admonished wags not to embroider on the tale. The oldtimers, however, didn't seem to think so. A few weeks later, they re-elected him by a landslide.

# Thirteen Ways of Looking at a Black Hole

## Or, Everything You Always Wanted to Know About Black Holes
## (But Were Too Dumb to Ask)

*"In the first year of the period Chih-ha, the fifth moon, the day Chi-chou, a great star appeared approximately several inches southeast of T'ien Kuan. After more than a year, it gradually became invisible."*

—annals of the Peiping Obeservatory

## I

An old high school classmate of mine, David Berlucki, was the first to tell me about black holes. It should have been another classmate, Juan Crisostomo Bernardo, whom we called Pocholo, because Cholo was always the first to know about such things, but it was definitely Dave this time. Cholo was our frontrunner: Best Debater, Student Council President, poet, linguist, math whiz, all-around egghead. He wound up valedictorian, for which he got a gold medal. Three other medals were for top grades in the major subjects: First in English, Second in Physics, Second in Mathematics. Dave was salutatorian, Second in English, First in Physics, First in Math. Two gold medals, two silver. Same count as Cholo's. We had expected Cholo to walk away with all three Firsts, but Dave had come from behind to grab his fair share of the gold. This left Antonino "Panikoy" Borromeo and Edmund "Teddy" Bagaman picking up the bronze medals after Bernardo and Berłucki. The four B's, we called them. They were a legend even then. They kept up a four-way fight for honors for all four of our high school years. However, Panikoy and Teddy were leading Thespians; they starred in too many productions to keep up with Cholo and Dave in the heavy subjects. As for me, I didn't get any medals but wasn't so bad at those subjects myself. I could hold my own.

We first discussed black holes as Boy Scouts gunning for the merit badge in Astronomy. This was in Cebu City's Sacred Heart School for Boys, a Jesuit-ran private school. The Society had always been more inclined to astronomy than most. Fr. Mena, our examiner, liked to tell us about such Jesuit astronomers as Schall von Bell, Boscovich, Padre Faura, etc. Even now, I can still recall that Johann Adam Schall von Bell, S.J., in Peking in 1630, revised the Chinese calendar at the Emperor's request. Twenty years previously, in 1610, the astrologers at the Ming court had erred in their forecast of a solar eclipse. The Son of Heaven executed them and remembered that the late graduate theologian Li Ma Tou, whose real name was Mateo Ricci, S.J., had been something of an astronomer. Ricci was one of the first missionaries to enter China and carry on from the unfulfilled dream of Francis Xavier, S.J. Ricci had written his Superior-General in Rome for a priest-astronomer before he died in

1609, but it took the Vatican two decades before they sent the German.

Roger Boskovich, S.J., or Ruggiero Boscovich, S.J., was actually Rudjer Josip Boskovič, S.J. It was easy to guess that Ricci was Italian and St. Francis Xavier Spanish, but only Dave guessed that Boskovic was Dalmatian. He of course had a dog of that breed. "Boskovič" had an accent called the hachek over the *c*, which gave that letter the *tch* sound. Dave's own name, Berłucki, had a barred *l* and a *ck* which in Polish took the values of *w* and of *tsk*, so his name was pronounced Berwootski. We had at first thought that "Berłucki" would rhyme with "very lucky". Some of us pronounced it Berlokoy to make it sound like "kolokoy," Visayan slang for "crazy fool." Soon we were calling him Bercootskin.

Boskovič in the 1740's measured the sun's equator, studied the aurora borealis, and observed transits of Mercury. I had to ask Dave where Dalmatia was. Cholo said it was now part of Yugoslavia. Boskovic, who died in 1787, spent most of his life in Pavia, Paris and Rome. Cholo wondered if Boskovič's work when Professor of Mathematics at the University of Pavia had helped lead Herschel to the discovery of Uranus in 1781. Fr. Mena said he wasn't sure, but he didn't think so.

Federico Faura, S.J., a Spaniard, was the director of the Observatorio Meteorologico de Manila from its founding in 1865 until his death in 1897. Padre Faura studied the stars and planets and attempted predictions of earthquakes and typhoons. He also measured surface ozone and its depletion. Stratospheric ozone, Fr. Mena told us, blocked out ultraviolet rays. Its depletion would lead to increased rates of skin cancer. Surface ozone was different. In excessive levels it was harmful not only to vegetation but also to human health, as it irritated the mucous membranes. Padre Faura's measurements of surface ozone levels, which he found to be steadily decreasing, were produced photochemically through a series of reactions involving carbon monoxide, methane, nonmethane hydrocarbons and nitrogen oxides.

Fr. Mena liked discussing with us, whenever our Literature teacher Mrs. Luab was around, the poetry of the Englishmen, Gerard Manley Hopkins, S.J., and the martyred Edmund Campion, S.J.

We heard so much about great Jesuits that Boojie Lim came up with this story: a Franciscan, a Dominican, and a Jesuit are all engaged in a mighty polemic. Each claims that his religious order is the best. Unable to settle the question, they write a letter to Heaven. A reply duly arrives. They should not waste time arguing about such things, the letter says, as their orders are all equally good. Each serves the Cause in its own way. Signed, Jesus Christ, S.J.

For our Astronomy merit badge exam, Fr. Mena took us up to the skytop of Sacred Heart's Luym Building one evening. He took the waterproof cover off the telescope mount, unlocked a cabinet, brought out the telescope, and attached it to the mount. A refractor, the telescope was about four feet long. It had a small aimer above it, like the telescopic sight on a rifle (it even had crosshairs) and coarse and fine adjustments on two axes. I don't remember its power or its focal length or whether it was equatorial- or azimuth-mounted. But it could show the rings of Saturn, the Galilean moons of Jupiter, and the phases of Venus. It could show the Crab Nebula, which we knew was the debris of a supernova first seen by the Chinese on July 4, 1054 AD, near the star Zeta

Tauri. ("*In...Chih-ha, the fifth moon, the day Chi-chou, a great star appeared...southeast of T'ien Kuan.*") It could show the Horsehead Nebula in Orion's sword. It could show the craters and mountains of the moon. I was much impressed by the bright splash rays of the crater Tycho.

Sántos González Mena, S.J., was a Spaniard who before becoming a priest had been a soldier, like Ignatius de Loyola himself. Iñigo Lopez de Rescalde had fought for the viceroy of Navarre against the French at the siege of Pamplona in 1521. Sántos González fought for the losing side in the Spanish Civil War. Just as Lopez de Rescalde changed his name to Loyola (his hometown), so too did González switch to his mother's name and become Mena. He would discuss art sometimes, and talk about Picasso, Miro or Dali, but would not talk about Franco. He also considered Elcano the first circumnavigator, not Magallanes. Once we asked him what he thought about Catalan nationalism and Basque separatism. Picasso after all was a Catalan; Loyola and Elcano were Basques. But he merely grunted. He pointed at our drawings.

"What is this crater called?"

"Kepler, Father."

"Correct. Now, who was Kepler?"

"Kepler said that the orbits of the planets were not circular. They were elliptical."

"Which satellites are these?"

"This is Ganymede, Father. And these are Europa, Io and Callisto."

And so on. Fr. Mena grilled us thoroughly but we had done our homework and we obviously shared his love for astronomy. We turned to joking about black holes while taking turns at the eyepiece. "There's a black hole!" Dave cried. Black holes, of course, were invisible. "It's sucking in a nebula!" Cholo said. I looked. The telescope was focused on the galaxy called Messier 33. (We grouped the galaxies, behind Fr. Mena's back, into three types: Messy, Messier, and Messiest.) It didn't look very interesting. Just a hazy swarm of stars. "There's twenty galaxies out there," I said, "and the black hole's eating them all up!"

Black holes probably did not exist. "They're a crazy idea those physicists cooked up," Fr. Mena said as he locked the telescope up in its cabinet. He had learned his English in the United States, four years at Georgetown University. Despite his ineradicable Spanish accent his English was as colloquial as Dave's or, for that matter, Cholo's and mine. "They mess around with Einstein's theories," Fr. Mena said, "and come up with all sorts of nonsense. I don't care if the math shows that black holes are possible in theory. There are many ways of solving those equations. But use your common sense. Can a whole star really collapse into a black hole?"

But that was just it. We had studied the idea, even tried out some of the math. If we had stuck to common sense alone, it might have told us that the world was flat. The mathematics predicted the black hole absolutely. There was no getting around it. Learning about the black hole had been a revelation; the concept moved us profoundly.

Among twenty milky nebulae, it was the only moving thing.

# II

I was of three minds, like the family tree of the black hole's theory.

"There are three possibilities," Dave said, apropos of stars dying. "If it's a small star, it collapses into a white dwarf. If it's a medium star, it blows up as a supernova and then condenses, what's left of it, into a neutron star. And if it's a big star, it becomes a black hole."

"A white dwarf," Cholo said, "is packed as tight as its electrons can allow. There's a limit to that, because they repel each other."

"Pauli's exclusion principle," I put in.

"Yes," Cholo said. "In the neutron star the electrons get squashed into the nucleus. Pauli's principle still applies, only this time the repulsion is between the protons and neutrons." Cholo at that time was working on his Physics term paper. It was on quantum mechanics. (Mine was on the Great Pyramid at Giza, and how the math involved in designing it seemed to imply knowledge of the earth's polar diameter and its orbital period.)

"In the black hole," Dave said, "gravitational collapse overcomes all the repulsive forces. All the star's matter, all its protons, neutrons, positrons, electrons and quarks, these all converge into a *single point*."

"In the Euclidean sense?" I asked.

"One single dimensionless point," Dave nodded.

"Meaning zero volume," Cholo said.

"Oh, come on," I said, "that's nuts."

"A feat of magic," Cholo said, "or a triumph of the imagination. Hard to tell which, hey?"

"It's got to be true," Dave said.

"It's just a lot of math, like Fr. Mena says," Cholo said. "Have they actually seen one?"

"Nothing yet," Dave said. "There's some likely ones, though. Cygnus X-1, f'rinstance. The quasar 3C273. It's pretty hard to explain these phenomena if they don't include black holes."

"Phenomena for Fr. Mena," I said. *"Parerga und Paralipomena."*

## III

The black hole whirled in the autumn sky. It was a small part of the universe. Cholo said the universe was a pantomime. "Because sound doesn't carry in space?" I asked. "No," he said, "it's a mime in math. Theories of the universe aren't done by philosophers anymore, like Aristotle, or the Brahmins of India who said that worlds are the backs of huge turtles. Nowadays models of the universe come from theories that involve a lot of math. You might say that all this math is a pantomime of the universe."

Dave was more practical about his math and his physics. They were what he would need most in college. He was going to take up Engineering. That was what you took if you were going to be a pilot. Dave planned to go to the US Air Force Academy in Colorado. His father being from Wisconsin (his mother was a Corominas of Cebu), Dave had dual citizenship. If the senior Senator from Wisconsin, William Proxmire, would appoint him to the Academy, Dave would give up the Filipino half.

Dave was a second-generation American, his father having been born in Wisconsin shortly after the Berłuckis got there from Poland. Dave was the kind who liked to send cards for Christmas and for birthdays, and it irked him no end that the Iron Curtain made it hard to keep in touch with his relatives. They lived in places like Bydgoszcz, Szczecin and Przemysl, and replies to his cards took forever. Once in a while a letter would get through and he would show it to us. "Where's it from?" we loved asking. "Szczecin," Dave would say, and one of us would repeat, dumb as you please, "Shit-ish-a-sin?"

Dave's father had been in the USAF. He got assigned to Clark, went to Cebu on R&R, and married a Corominas lady. He was an all-American guy, as were his sons. It wasn't hard to stay all-American in Cebu if you lived in an exclusive neighborhood and went to the best schools. Everyone spoke good English at Sacred Heart, even the ethnic Chinese who made up some two-thirds of our class. The Spanish meztisos, about 15% of us, still swore in Spanish but spoke mostly in Californese. The remainder, guys of Malay stock like me, spoke Visayan, English and Tagalog, and learned to swear in English, Spanish and Chinese—Fukienese, that is. Many of my classmates traced their roots to Amoy, which they did not like to call Xiamen in the Mandarin way. Every year we would get two or three new classmates from Cantonese-speaking families. These boys were invariably nicknamed "Macao."

Dave could swear in Polish. It sounded like Russian to us so we always swore back at him in B-movie German. After a couple of grading periods Dave became good at swearing in Chinese, thanks to the efforts of Roy Emil Yu and Henry Tanchan.

Senator Proxmire's appointment of Berłucki to the US Air Force Academy was contingent upon the latter's grades. This was what drove Dave to catch up and wrest two of the four gold medals we had virtually conceded to Cholo. Cholo did his best to stay ahead, but his goal looked somewhat less exalted: a scholarship at the Ateneo de Manila. He did all the math required in our curriculum and then some, only to find that Dave had gone deeper. Dave had plunged right into the Schwarzschild and the Kerr solutions of the field equations in Einstein's general theory of relativity. This was the math the theoretical physicists used when they talked about black holes. It was way above my level. I couldn't follow the mathematical reasoning that proved black holes were spherical. The math even proved that if a black hole were rotating, it would bulge at the equator just as our planet does. Great math, elegant solutions. What the heck. I didn't even try. Einstein's $E = mc^2$ was about as much as I could handle.

Dave could put an equation through its paces as efficiently as Jeffrey Dico, the corps commander of our PMT unit, could dismantle a Colt .45 while blindfolded. Joe "90" Soberano (the nickname expressed his height in centimeters) loved going to the blackboard before the teacher arrived so he could pantomime Dave solving an equation. Joe would raise a fylfot to the $n$th exponent or extract the square root of a Greek letter. He would divide ideograms by zero to get infinity. He would scribble things like

$$n + \varepsilon^2 = \delta/\clubsuit$$

or something like

$$\zeta(\varsigma) = \Sigma \kappa^{-3} (\Re \varsigma > 1)$$
$$\kappa = 1$$

with the summation from $\kappa=1$ to $\infty$.

or even something really outrageous like

$$\delta s^2 = c^2 \gamma \delta t^2 - r^2 (\delta \theta^2 + \sin^2 \theta \delta \phi^2) - \gamma^{-1} \delta r^2$$
$$\gamma = 1 - 2kn/rc^2$$

We always found it hilarious. Joe had Dave's mannerisms down pat, even the way he whirled. It was a small part of the pantomime.

## IV

A swan and a woman are one. Cygnus and Leda and the black hole are X-1.

"Cygnus X-1 is a binary system," Dave said. "Two stars orbiting each other. Only one of them is visible, the lighter one. You can estimate its mass easily enough, and its orbit. From that you can figure out the lowest possible mass of its invisible, and heavier, partner. Here it's way above the Chandrasekhar Limit, so logically it must be a black hole."

"Why don't they declare it as such?" I asked.

"Too far away. They can't be positive about it."

"Science would have us believe it's a black hole," Cholo said, "just as myth or religion told the ancients that Cygnus was Jupiter disguised as a swan. What's more, this swan made it with Leda. I don't know who's got to make the more fearful leap into the dark, us or the ancients."

## V

I do not know which to prefer, the beauty of equations, or the beauty of unsettled bets; the black hole collapsing, or just before.

Einstein's equations, Cholo said, were as elegant as Ramanujan's theorems. Srinavasa Ramanujan was the unknown Indian from the Madras hinterland who, in 1913, sent a letter to G.H. Hardy, the head of the Mathematics Department at Cambridge University in England. The letter contained 120 original theorems. Hardy suspected it was just another crank letter. Upon scrutiny, however, the theorems turned out to be truly brilliant and original. Hardy decided they had to be true, because if they were not, "no one would have the imagination to invent them." Ramanujan was a genius who had sprung out of nowhere. A few of his theorems were already well known in the West; Ramanujan had discovered them again all by himself, further proof of his genius.

For our math class several of us submitted, in lieu of the usual term paper, proofs of a Ramanujan theorem. Our math teacher, Mr. Goyangco, made sure we all worked on different theorems. Proving just one theorem was hard work, about as hard as doing a term paper. It gave us a new taste for math, and soon we spent our study periods discussing each other's proofs. That was when Dave sprung the Schwarzschild solution of Einstein's equations on us. It showed that a black hole must be perfectly spherical. Dave followed it up with the Kerr solution. This one showed that a black hole was spherical only if nonrotating. If it did rotate, it would bulge at its equator. We didn't understand at first. We didn't know what he could mean by the "car solution." Dave explained that Einstein published his equations in 1905, astronomer Karl Schwarzschild of Potsdam did his solution of them in 1916, and mathematician Roy Kerr of New Zealand in 1963. It was all math. Applying this math to the theory of the black hole had been done between 1967 and 1971 by theorists like Werner Israel, Brandon Carter and Stephen Hawking. In 1969 physicist John Wheeler had coined the term "black hole."

"Hey, Dave," Cholo said, "bet you black holes don't exist."

"Oh, yeah, wanna bet? How much?"

"My Apollo models against your polaroids."

"Okay, you're on."

Cholo had models of the Apollo command and lunar modules he'd put together from a kit. Dave had a pair of polarized USAF-issue aviator sunglasses. They were a hand-me-down from his elder brother, but Joe Soberano said Dave had probably bought them in Dau, Pampanga, the previous summer vacation.

Years later I learned that Stephen Hawking of Cambridge and Kip Thorne of Cal Tech had made a similar wager. If black holes did not exist Hawking's lifework would go down the drain, but he would win a four-year subscription to *Private Eye* magazine. If black holes were real, Hawking would lose the bet and have to pay Thorne a year of *Penthouse*.

Both bets, as far as I know, remain unsettled. Hawking recently said astronomers were now 99% convinced Cygnus X-1 includes a black hole, but it would take 100% to lose that bet. I had thought it would suffice merely to

observe a big star that was dying and then, after its collapse, verify that nothing remained. That would be a black
hole. No light could escape its gravity, no information.
But stars live for millions of years. None of them so far
has been very obliging.

## VI

Gamma rays filled the launch window with barbaric
bursts. It was the black hole. Dave sought it still, quested
for it beyond the wild blue yonder. Beyond the Milky Way.

*"Oh, I have slip'd the surly bonds of earth,"* he must have
lipsynched to himself, inside his helmet, the first time he
attained orbital velocity. Even if only in a dream. What
he actually said was: "It really looks great from up here.
There's the Philippines, where I lived as a boy. Lots of
clouds over it, but I can make out the island of Cebu.
Wow, I didn't know it could look so beautiful. It's just
fantastic, Houston."

His first space flight and he was the pilot, second in
command. The commander was the veteran astronaut
Karol Bobko. Two Poles piloting the shuttle *Atlantis*. And
one of them a Visayan Pole. Both of them all-American.
I'd learned the names of the crew a few days before,
from a newspaper. Flights of the NASA shuttles rated
two or three sentences these days, mostly about the mission objectives. This particular news item happened to
include the crew roster, for once. Commander, pilot, two
mission specialists, two payload specialists. Two Poles,
Bobko and Berłucki. A Navajo Indian and a white woman,
Sidney "El Kidney" Gutiérrez and Tamara Jernigan. A black
woman and a New Orleans creole, Mae Jemison and Pierre
Thuot.

So Dave had made astronaut. News about him had been desultory over the years, filtering down through ex-classmates here and there. Proxmire's appointment had come through and Dave had gone to Colorado. We all knew that. USAF Academy in Rampart Range, with some of their classes at Lowry AFB in Denver. There was the time Chi Chi Villarica said one of the Corominas girls, cousin to Dave, had shown him a picture of Dave posing in front of a T-38. Dave was flying supersonic as an undergraduate. That was the US Air Force for you. Fighter pilots of Third World countries, by contrast, could expect to fly supersonic only as postgraduate fellows, if at all.

Next we heard, 2nd Lt. Berłucki was in an F-15 squadron based in Ramstein, West Germany. I wondered if Dave ever managed to violate East German airspace. He might have gone supersonic at 30,000 feet and taken only a few minutes to reach Poland, whose soil his ancestors had tilled and perhaps shed their blood for. I knew I would have, given the slightest excuse. But I doubted if Dave was that sentimental a fool, even if he felt good enough to outfight a MiG-27 or two.

Dave left his gold bar in Deutschland with some blonde *fraulein* and went back to the US wearing the silver bar of a First Lieutenant. He got an MA in Astronautics at MIT on a Rhodes Engineering Scholarship. From there, it was test pilot school, or Aerospace Research Pilot School, at Edwards in California. Muroc Dry Lake, he called it. Just like the old hands did. Unconfirmed rumor claimed that Dave once briefly waxed Brig. Gen. Chuck Yeager's tail in an impromptu mock dogfight.

They no longer flew the X-15 at Edwards but Capt. Berłucki was on hand to watch astronauts Young and

Crippen land the shuttle *Columbia* at the end of her maiden voyage. That was in 1981. I was getting along fine, although my math had gone rusty. I could barely fathom the arguments that a black hole must emit X-rays and gamma rays. Emit? Wasn't supposed to do that, was it? A black hole's gravity was supposed to be so absolute that nothing could escape from it. Not even light. How could it emit X-rays and gamma rays?

Two Soviet scientists, Zeldovich and Starobinsky, were saying that rotating black holes should emit those particles, if only to avoid violating the second law of thermodynamics. I couldn't even remember how that law went. Hawking didn't like their math so he went over it and devised a better approach. Surprise, surprise. His math showed that even nonrotating black holes emitted particles. I wondered if Dave or Cholo was following all this. Their math would have coped. Mine couldn't, not anymore. My life was getting full of moods and shadows, and the black hole to me now traced an indecipherable cause. It crossed my shadows, to and fro.

# VII

O tin man of Kalusuan, why do you imagine doughnut holes in Butuan? Do you not see how the black hole is smaller than the island around your feet?

Kalusuan was the smallest island any of us high school seniors had ever seen. We were standing at its center. Cholo pivoted a full 360 degrees and noted that the sea was visible whichever direction you faced. It seemed as if a strong wave could loose Kalusuan from its moorings and set us adrift.

"Since we're here on Kalusuan," said Raymund "Loki" Fernandez, "let's take that pumpboat and sail to Butuan."

He pronounced both placenames the old way. This gave them, to a Visayan ear, prurient meanings. The male sense of it attached to Kalusuan, the female sense to Butuan, so it was natural to suggest a trip between the two. Raymund, the only one of us who had read the *Kama Sutra*, liked saying such things when he was high. Now he started strumming his guitar.

> *Well, Oz never did give nuthin' to the tin man,*

he sang,

> *That he didn't, didn't already have...*

Dave went off for a swim with Joe and Panikoy. Cholo and Teddy were minding the barbecue. Joel Ramos took another puff, then passed me the reefer. Way to go, baby. No teachers, just us. We were high school seniors. We owned the world.

Tony Cabinian, whose mother was the Anita of Anita's Bakeshop, passed a bag of doughnuts around. "Hey, eye-diots," he yelled to the swimmers, "doughnuts!"

He pronounced "idiots" as "eye-diots" because we had recently acquired a rookie teacher who pronounced it that way.

"Hey, Dave," Cholo called out, "you still say black holes exist?"

"Why, sure they do," Dave said, struggling with Panikoy and Joe for the bag of doughnuts. Joe was hugging the bag to his chest and wolfing down three doughnuts at once.

"Well," Cholo said, "a black hole is just like this dough-nut hole, then."

"How's that?" Dave asked.

"It's not a doughnut without the hole, see? But you don't eat the hole. So when you've eaten the doughnut, does the hole still exist or not?"

We all burst out in loud guffaws. Dave picked up two sticks of barbecue from the grill. They were done. He handed one to Cholo. Then he lunged at him, and the two of them began fencing, using the sticks like rapiers. With both sticks full of smoking meat, fat dripping, they looked ridiculous and we kept on laughing. Dave found an opening, made a good clean thrust. Rather a gentle one, I thought. Cholo looked stunned, then drew back, fist cocked. A spot of blood appeared on his bare chest. Now we're in for a real fight, I thought. Everyone was suddenly quiet. Cholo was no wimp, despite his thick glasses. But Dave, who was on the soccer team, certainly looked more fit.

Ulysses Yap stepped in, still laughing.

"Okay, Cholo," he said, "you made your point. Now Dave's made his."

Cholo wiped the blood off his chest with his thumb. "You forgot to say it, Dave."

"Say what?"

"*Touché*."

# VIII

We knew the Nobel accents of lucid, inescapable theo-ries. And the ones that came before. Those were high school lessons for us. Names matched themselves with theories, in our young minds, at a snap of the fingers. Aristotle: that the universe was made of four elements, earth, wind, fire and water. Democritus: that it was made up of atoms. Ptolemy: that the earth was the center of the universe, and everything revolved around it on celestial spheres. Then Copernicus, Kepler, Newton: the heliocentric system, elliptical orbits, gravity. After them we could spout a list of names not so well known, most of them Nobel Prize winners. Michelson, who took the measure of light. Thomson, Lord Rutherford, Chadwick, Dirac, Gell-Mann. Discoverers of the atom's components: of the electron, the proton, the neutron, the positron. All of which were, in turn, made up of quarks. Cholo told us to pronounce it "quarts" because he knew where the word came from. It was from a line in *Finnegans Wake*, the James Joyce novel, "Three quarks for Muster Mark!" Probably a typo, of course, making it two typos in that single line. Quarks came in six "flavors" and each flavor had three "colors." Murray Gell-Mann, who got a Nobel in 1969 for discovering quarks, must have loved ice cream.

Max Planck got a Nobel in 1918, for the quantum theory, of course. Einstein got his in 1933, no need to ask what it was for. Wolfgang Pauli got one in 1945, for the exclusion principle in subatomic particles. And there was Subramanyan Chandrasekhar. We wondered why he hadn't been given a Nobel. His fine work of 1928 had been gladsome toil, calculating that a massive star at death would collapse into a zero-volume singularity. His mentor at Cambridge, Eddington, would not accept that result. Einstein himself, whose equations had given Chandrasekhar a starting point, said he doubted if shrinking to zero volume was possible. Chandrasekhar was persuaded to turn to other lines of work. In 1983 I was pleasantly surprised to hear he was being awarded a Nobel Prize, even if it was for his work on galaxies. Belated, I thought, for a man who told us about the fates of stars.

"When a small star dies," Cholo observed, "it goes to white-dwarf heaven. For every seven white dwarfs, there must be a singularity named Snow White.

"Other stars, when they die, purge off their excess matter by exploding as supernovae. Then their cores contract into dark stars: neutron stars, pulsars or quasars. They're in Purgatory.

"When a big star dies it becomes a black hole, from which there is no escape. Light can't escape its gravity, and time itself stops. Inside a black hole, everything is frozen in a moment of forever. A black hole is Hell. Dante was misled by Ptolemy. He thought Hell had nine circles, like celestial spheres. That can't be right. Hell is a single point. Hell is a black hole."

"Tell that to Fr. Mena, Cholo," Montxu Aboitiz said.

"No, Cholo wouldn't dare," Teofilo Uy said.

"I would, too," Cholo said. "There's only one thing I wouldn't dare tell Fr. Mena, and that's Tim's joke about the S.J."

"How does that go?" Henry "Het-het" Pelaez asked.

"Yeah, c'mon, Timothy," Montxu said, "tell us about the S.J. Don't be shy, jake."

"Okay," Timothy Dunque said, "you know, when Jesus was born, He was lying there in that manger. He opened His eyes and looked around Him. To His right was a donkey and to His left, an ass. So He asked: 'Is this the society of Jesus?'"

We laughed. Then Dave spoke up.

"Let's not get heaven and hell into it, guys. Cholo, we've been talking about only one kind of black hole. What about the other kind?"

"Oh, I'd forgotten all about that, Dave. Let me see, ah, primordial black hole, wasn't it?"

I was astounded. These guys meant there wasn't one but two kinds of black holes. And it sounded like Dave had just found out about the second type. Nobody else could have heard about it yet. But Cholo already knew! That was truly astounding.

"Yeah, well," Dave said, "you must all have heard about it, what Hawking's been theorizing about." He was talking to Tim and to me. But Cholo wouldn't be put off so easily.

"A black hole," Cholo recited, "can be formed by the gravitational collapse of a massive star, one that exceeds the Chandrasekhar Limit." He made it sound like a line in a textbook.

"But," and here Cholo started chewing on his plastic ballpen cap, a mannerism that disgusted Dave, "it's just possible that stars below the Chandrasekhar Limit could have been compressed into black holes. Not by their own gravity. By external pressure."

"Hawking thinks such pressures," Dave said, "would have been possible only at the birth of the universe."

"If we assume," I put in, "that it started with the Big Bang."

"Of course," Cholo said.

"So," Dave said, "if we can find these primordial black holes, they could tell us something about conditions that existed at the Big Bang."

"Nanoseconds," Cholo said, "into the Big Bang. At Planck Time, which is $10^{-43}$ of a second after the Big Bang."

"These would be mini black holes," Dave said, "with masses below the Chandrasekhar Limit. They should have become stars, candidates for white dwarfism, but got imploded by external pressure into black holes. To use your terms, Cholo, they should have gone to Heaven but instead got kicked down into Hell."

"Like fallen angels," Cholo said.

"How small would they be?" I asked.

"Just as small, actually," Dave said. "Zero volume. But less massive, a lot less. Hawking thinks they'd each be worth about ten billion tons of matter. That's the mass of a small mountain on this planet."

"The less massive the black hole," Cholo said, "the more X-rays and gamma rays it emits, because it's all inversely proportional. How much energy would it release, Dave?"

"Oh, maybe ten thousand megawatts, I don't know."

"That's a lot of energy," Cholo said. "The typical American nuclear plant yields only a thousand. Could that be harnessed?"

"Perhaps. I wouldn't know how. One thing for sure, not on earth, I mean not on the surface. Hawking thinks the only way is to keep it in orbit."

"Yes, of course," Cholo said. "All that mass concentrated in something like the head of a pin. No, smaller. The nucleus of an atom, maybe."

"How many angels could dance on a black hole?" I asked.

"One, maybe," Dave said. "Two if it's a slow drag they're dancing."

"As I was saying," Cholo said, "all that concentrated mass would sink right through the earth. All the way to the center, right, Dave?"

"All the way to the other side," Dave said. "We put it on Kalusuan Island it'd come out somewhere in Brazil. Then it would sink right back and, like, oscillate back and forth until it settled at the center."

"And there," I said, surprised at my own revelation, "its gravity would suck everything in. The earth would get suckered in until all its matter went into the black hole."

"So we keep it in orbit," Cholo said.

"Where we can figure out how to harness its energy," Dave said, "and study it for insights into the Big Bang."

"I still say heck, let's drop it on Kalusuan," I said.

"Right," Cholo agreed. "all things considered."


Primordial black holes would confirm the Big Bang and perhaps bring us closer to the Grand Unified Theory. This was the elusive theory that would reconcile Einstein's relativity with quantum mechanics. We knew this. We wondered if Stephen Hawking, afflicted with amyotropic lateral sclerosis or Lou Gehrig's disease, wheelchair-bound, vocal cords gone after a bout of pneumonia and

able to talk only through a computerized speech synthe-
sizer, divorced from the wife who had borne him three
children and now married to his nurse—we wondered if
Stephen Hawking would be the one to come up with
the Grand Unified Theory.

We knew about Edwin Hubble, the first to look for
distant galaxies. He found them, measured their red
shifts, and in 1929 reported that the universe was expanding. Everybody knew about Hubble. But we also
knew about Aleksandr Friedmann, the Russian mathematician who made a model of the universe based on
Einstein's equations. His model showed an expanding
universe. Friedmann thus anticipated, in 1922, what
Hubble published in 1929.

We knew too that Einstein himself had been unpre-
pared for a dynamic, expanding universe. Men had always thought of the universe as static, unchanging, eter-
nal. As late as the early sixties, astronomers like Fred
Hoyle still clung to the "steady state" universe. Einstein
went out of his way to introduce a "cosmological constant" so that his equations would still yield a static universe. Friedmann ignored that constant. Hubble's findings showed it was unnecessary. Einstein later called that
constant his "biggest mistake."

Dave summed it all up in his term paper. His con-
cluding paragraph I can still quote verbatim:

"In this century, within the lifetime of a man my
grandfather's age, our concept of the universe has been
radically changed. Now we know it began with a Big
Bang, and is still expanding. Hawking tells us the expan-
sion will stop someday, and the process go into reverse.
Then the universe will contract. The end of it will be the

Big Crunch, when all the matter in the universe collapses into a single black hole."

This was a lucid, inescapable theory, indeed. We knew it. And the black hole was involved in what we knew.

# IX

When the black hole shrank out of sight, it marked the edge of its one and only event horizon.

A pair of particles, a quark and an antiquark, formed near the event horizon. Normally such matter-antimatter pairs would be fated to reunite and thus annihilate each other. In this case however, the antiquark entered the boundary and was sucked into the black hole. The quark escaped. "To an observer at a distance," Hawking had said, "it will appear to have been emitted from the black hole."

"We may detect a black hole," Dave was saying, "by its Hawking radiation."

"So the black hole," Cholo said, "doth hawk its wares."

"This radiation," Dave went on, "usually in the form of gamma rays, marks the edge of the black hole's event horizon..."

"Same old Dave," Cholo said. I took a swig of beer. We were older somehow, college was behind us, we were breeding smart-alecky kids, high school seemed so long ago. We were in Cholo's living room, watching Dave on TV. Cholo had a few things I didn't have, a personal computer with a modem, fax, and CD-ROM, the whole thing linked to the Internet. He also had a slew of sophisticated radio and video equipment and his own dish antenna. An uncle of his had once been a ham radio whiz, and Cholo had learned a few tricks from him, such as figuring out the secret frequencies manned spacecraft used and tuning in to them. I'd come over to catch the transmission from the shuttle *Atlantis*. Cholo had found the orbiter's frequency and knew how to combine its transmissions with the Internet coverage.

"Dave says his food's a bit different than the rest of the crew's," Cholo told me. "Says he's got *puso* and *ngo hiong*."

"From the NASA kitchens or smuggled aboard?"

"I don't know. I think he's putting us on. Isn't applesauce the only food they're allowed? Only thing that doesn't leave crumbs floating around in the cabin."

"Applesauce is from the Spam-in-a-can days of the Mercury astronauts. Nowadays they eat *à la carte*. Doesn't that black girl, Jemison, have soul food? And that New Orleans guy would have Cajun food. Gumbo and crayfish."

The camera panned to the rear window. The orbiter's manipulator arm came into view, "Canada" and a red maple leaf printed on it. If the Canadians had given it more thought they would have written it the other way around, so that it didn't always appear upside down.

Two astronauts in pressure suits came floating out of the airlock. They were Jemison and Thuot, as Dave's voice-over told us, on EVA to retrieve a satellite. Dave's voice still had that Midwest twang we knew so well.

"Mission commander Karol Bobko is at the controls, and we've just completed the rendezvous. Carolus will maneuver *Atlantis* into position above the target satellite. We'll be upside down as viewed from earth, but of course here in space that doesn't matter. Mae and Pierre are outside now. They're strapped by their boots to the payload bay's edge. Take it easy now, Mae, Pierre. We don't want you floating away. Pierre's gonna grab the target when it gets close and Mae will grab his feet if he floats off with the satellite. Isn't that how you two are working it?"

"Not quite, Dave," Thuot chuckled. His voice had a faint French accent. "We're gonna pull ourselves up by the bootstraps. Then I'm gonna use this here rope that I brought along. I'm gonna lasso it in."

"Y'all heard him," Jemison said. "We gonna bust this ol' bronco jes' lahk the man sez."

"Aren't they mixing their metaphors?" I asked Cholo.

"I guess they're allowed to do that. At least they no longer say 'beautiful' and 'fantastic' four times each every other sentence."

"Betcha some of them will still say 'piece of cake'."

"Not these folks. Only guest astronauts would say that. Not the ones with the right stuff."

## X

At the sight of black holes sucking in all their red light, even the lords of astronomy would cry out sharply.

"*Mamma mia!*" Galileo would say. "*Eppur si muove. Magnifico!*"

"Do the fandango!" Scaramouche would say.

"*Ist das wirlich so?*" Einstein would say.

"*Karrat putschzhinckheit!*" Juaniyo Arcellana would say.

"*Ya gah wei, la!*" Cholo said. He hadn't forgotten how to swear in Chinese. We were at his personal computer.

Cholo was good at doing graphics, and he had just simulated the collapse of a dying star into a black hole.

He started with a red giant, programmed to become a black hole at T-0. At T minus 3 it was still a red giant, light rays from it still travelling to us. One second later, at T minus 2, no apparent changes. Another second went by. It was at T minus 1, with still no changes, only now time seemed to be slowing down; more than one second elapsed between T-2 and T-1. From T-1 to T-0 seemed forever. The elapsed time between successive waves of light was getting longer. The light waves were getting stretched, reaching more and more into the red wavelengths. The star was getting redder and redder, and also fainter and fainter. There is no sound in space, but it seemed to be whistling. And then it was gone.

It looked so much like the real thing we both cried out sharply, reflexively. "Holy shit!" I said.

"*Bilang sa kagang*," Cholo whispered, in a rural accent.

# XI

They flew over Dinagat in the shuttle *Atlantis*. Once a fear gripped them, in that they mistook the shadow of their equipage for black holes.

"Black holes in the ozone layer," astronaut Tamara Jernigan said. "While they're fixing that bucking bronco satellite of theirs, I'm using different kinds of cameras to photograph the ozone layer. The holes in it seem to be getting bigger."

"Sure that's a hole?" astronaut Sidney Gutiérrez asked. "Looks to me like our shadow."

"Oh, Sidney, you're a pain in the kidney."

Dave's voice: "How's it going, Mae and Pierre?"

"Copacetic, Dave," Thuot said. "One of the solar panels looks done for. We'll have to replace it. Of the four gyros only one remains operative. We'll replace three. Then we'll install a new planetary widefield camera. We'll also upgrade the computer by equipping it with a new co-processor. Finally we'll put in the COSTAR. That stands for Corrective Optics Space Telescope Axial Replacement. It's a corrective lens, actually. It's the trickiest part of this job."

They were working on the Hubble Space Telescope. Shortly after reaching orbit three years before, it had become one of NASA's biggest embarrassments. The pictures it sent back were all blurred. The telescope's primary mirror had been ground to the wrong curvature. It was off by 0.000039 of an inch, a slight error that made all the difference. The blame was put on the computer program used to grind the mirror. Good policy: always blame the computer. Now *Atlantis* would remedy things. Bobko's crew had brought up a big lens that would compensate for the mirror's curvature and allow a really sharp focus.

"Wouldn't that lens," I asked Cholo, "introduce some chromatic aberration?"

"Around the edges, I guess," Cholo, said. "You remember what Newton said in his book *Opticks*? You know it can't be helped. But they've been computer-enhancing their blurred pictures. I suppose they'll handle the aberration with their standard deconvolution techniques."

Dave was back on live TV. The crew seem to have appointed him talk-show host for the duration. Four of them had doctorates, while Dave only had a master's degree. But he was the Rhodes scholar, as Hubble had been. Perhaps they deferred to this. Or was he just the best gabber?

"We're over the Philippines," Dave said. "Down there is the Visayas region, under all that cloud cover. I can see Dinagat Island though, in the Surigao Strait. I can see all the way to Thailand in the west, and there are the islands of Micronesia coming up in the east. Mae Jemison and Pierre Thuot are repressurizing in the airlock right now. The Hubble Telescope is in the payload bay awaiting further repair. They still have to put in that tricky corrective lens.

"For those of you who've just tuned in, I'd like to tell you a few basic things about the Hubble Space Telescope. It's about 44 feet long and 14 feet wide, and it's got solar panels that convert sunlight into electrical power. The panels look like wings. The Hubble always looks like it's flying. Now, this telescope was named after Edwin Hubble, the American astronomer who was the first to show that ours is not the only galaxy in the universe. Hubble began his search for distant galaxies in 1924, and he found hundreds of them. Today we think there must be millions of galaxies in our universe. Hubble catalogued what he found, estimated their distances from us, and analyzed their spectra. Today astronomers also analyze the periods of Cepheid variables to estimate distance, but this technique hadn't been invented in those days. Hubble found something strange: all the spectra had large shifts to the red end. He took this to mean, correctly, that all these galaxies were receding. And in 1929, when he announced his findings, he formulated the theory that's now known as the Big Bang.

"Edwin Hubble, using the 200-inch Hale reflector telescope at Mt. Palomar in California, was the first to look into the farthest reaches of the universe. It's fitting that this orbiting telescope is named after him, because the Hubble Telescope will allow us to see much farther into the universe than ever before. It'll give us a view right to the very edges. You see, by placing this telescope in orbit, we do away with the distortion caused by the earth's atmosphere. Up here where there's no air, the view is crystal clear. The Hubble has a reflecting mirror only 94 inches across. That's a lot smaller than the 200 inches of the Hale Telescope, or the 400 inches of that hexagonal Keck Telescope at Mauna Kea in Hawaii's Big Island. But it's still an improvement. Do you know how much of the energy coming from distant stars is absorbed by the atmosphere? Well, I'll tell you: it's ninety percent. That's a lot of energy, and it's all lost before it reaches earthbound telescopes. But the Hubble gets it all.

"The atmosphere, as you know, causes stars to twinkle. That's great for poets, but it's a headache for astronomers. Now, by staying in orbit 300 miles above the earth, the Hubble can see seven times as far as the Hale Telescope can. It can observe 350 times the volume of sky, and see objects 50 times dimmer than anything the Hale Telescope can pick up. The Hale Telescope at Mt. Palomar can see things two billion light-years away. The Hubble is much more farsighted. It can see objects 8 or 9 billion light-years away.

Since the Big Bang is thought to have taken place between 10 and 12 billion years ago, the Hubble can show us things that were happening when the universe was in its infancy.

"Now, I guess you know that when the Hubble Telescope was deployed by the shuttle *Discovery* in April 1990, we found a slight defect in it. The curvature of its mirror wasn't quite right. It hobbled the Hubble's vision. What we're attempting now is to correct this impairment by putting a lens called the COSTAR into the telescope. COSTAR stands for Corrective Optics Space Telescope Axial Replacement. It will put things in focus, and scientists will finally get that crystal-clear view they've been waiting for all these years.

"Payload specialists Pierre Thuot and Mae Jemison have begun their spacewalk now and soon COSTAR will be in place. It's an old-fashioned monocle, really. I think Pierre isn't sure how to put on that *pince-nez*. That's because he's never worn anything but contact lenses."

"*Touché*," interjected Pierre Thuot. Dave paused to acknowledge that, then resumed his talk:

"When the Hubble becomes operational again, astronomers will be able to see clearly into the beginnings of the universe. They'll look at Cepheid variables and estimate their distances from us. They'll probably also look for black holes. You see, black holes could tell us a lot about conditions that existed at the Big Bang. They might look at the double star Cygnus X-1, the quasar 3C273, or the galaxies called NGC 7457, NGC 4258, and Messier 87. These are among the likeliest places to look for black holes. Some people still think black holes don't exist but if they do, the Hubble just might find them. The Hubble Space Telescope will open up the universe to us, just as the first telescope opened up the sky to Galileo.

"This is the *Atlantis* coming to you live from over the island of St. Helena in the Atlantic. You know, that's where Napoleon died in 1821. On behalf of my crewmates Carolus Bobko, Sidney "El Kidney" Gutiérrez, Tamara Jernigan, Mae Jemison and Pierre Thuot, this is yours truly, Dave Berlucki. Thank you, *dobry wieczor*, and, ah, *magandang gabi, bayan*."

# XII

The universe is expanding. The black hole must be red-shifting. That is, if it had a spectrum to begin with. Were gamma rays and X-rays subject to the Doppler effect?

"Think they'll find a black hole?" Cholo asked me. "Now that the Hubble's been fixed?"

"No, I don't. The odds are against them. It might even out though, if, and only if, they had some Jesuit astronomer looking for it. Some latter-day Boskovič. Another Schall von Bell."

"Yeah, that's what they need."

"Have you heard from Fr. Mena lately? Where's he now?"

"Oh, I hear he's at Xavier U."

"In Cagayan de Oro?"

"No. The one in Manila. Supposedly he's close to proving Fermat's Last Theorem."

"Is he, now? And I always thought it was the Goldbach Conjecture he was working on. Well, how about another simulation on that computer of yours? I'd like to get a primordial into earth orbit. See if we can harness its energy."

Cholo took the cap off a plastic ballpen and chewed it ragged while his fingers deftly tapped out sequences on the keyboard. The technology required for the scheme belonged to the future, which didn't faze him at all. He simply factored in a lot of unknowns. The computer couldn't get that act together. The black hole in low orbit moved at 17,000 mph while a power station on the equator moved at 1,000. Cholo moved the black hole up to a circular orbit, concentric with the equator, 22,300 miles above the surface. There its orbital period was 24 hours, so it remained geostationary. He dragged and dropped a conduit in, resized and positioned it, and double-clicked. It worked fine. "That's the way to do it," Cholo said. "Money for nothing."

"All those megawatts for free," I said. "For our refrigerators. And our color TVs."

"The conduit's a given," Cholo said. "Looks too long to be practical."

"Let's quit while we're ahead."

"Hey, let's do what you always wanted to do. Let's drop that black hole on Kalusuan Island."

We had used a black hole with the volume of a pinhead. Now Cholo programmed one with zero volume.

"No go," he said after a few tries. "I think they put Einstein's cosmological constant into this computer. It can't deal with the Euclidean concept of a single, infinitely small, dimensionless point. I mean it can, but it won't put ten billion tons of mass into it."

"Ask it how many angels it can get to dance on the head of a pin."

"Sure. Give me an equation for angels."

Cholo factored another quantity in. Something clicked in the computer's circuitry, and all of a sudden there it was. The black hole was on Kalusuan Island. It sank immediately. It fell all the way to the center of the earth and then its momentum carried it almost to the surface on the other side, somewhere in the Brazilian rainforest. It didn't quite break the surface. The computer must have allowed for friction. It oscillated back and forth, falling and rising less and less each time, until it found equilibrium at the center.

"Won't its gravity suck the planet's matter in?" I asked.

"It might, but we've got to check these figures. It probably has a critical mass where it starts to do that."

Cholo switched to the Internet coverage, reducing the math display into a small window in a corner of the computer. He began tapping out equations. His math was too fast for me to follow. I didn't even try. The main display was too riveting, anyway.

"*...over Florida at 90,000. Still going like a dingbat. Atlantis, F-15 chase. How do you read me?*"

"*Read you six by six, chase. How me?*"

It was Bobko's voice. The shuttle was in flight, wheeling and doing S-turns. It dipped under the chase plane, and I saw the cloud cover far below. The F-15 obviously had a TV camera, and I was getting a pilot's-eye view of *Atlantis* coming home.

"*I make that St. Petersburg,*" Bobko said, "*and over there's Orlando.*"

I realized he meant the town of St. Pete in Florida. For a moment I had thought he meant the one in Russia, the one I still thought of as Leningrad.

"*There's the Cape,*" Dave's voice came over, "*and that lovely runway. Wonder how we're gonna get down? Looks like we could glide all the way to Timbuktu from here.*"

"*Let's go into that spiral staircase,*" Bobko said.

The shuttle's descent thrilled me. It went into a steep dive, turning in a wide spiral, less like a falling leaf than a rock caught in a tornado's downdraft. The F-15 followed, but didn't attempt to match the shuttle's rate of descent.

"*Flies real good,*" Bobko said, "*but needs a light touch. Try it, Dave. See?*"

The *Atlantis* climbed, dipped again, banked, then did a sideslip.

"*Hey, you're a hell of a glider pilot,*" Bobko said. "*Loved that sideslip. Where'd you learn how to do that?*"

"*Always wanted to try one,*" Dave said. "*Never could do that in the simulator.*"

"*Know what, guys who got a heavy hand can find this bird flying like a duck,*" Bobko said. "*A duck with a brick tied to its ass.*"

*Atlantis* was still coming down at a 20° angle. Then, at what must have been 1,000 feet, it pulled into a tight turn to intercept a very gentle 1½° glide path. It was on final approach.

"*I know that turn was only one and three-quarter G's,*" Bobko said, "*but it sure felt like six.*"

"*You're not gonna black out now, are you?*" Dave asked.

"*Nah. Us dumb Polacks only black out vhen ve drink too much fodka.*"

*"Speed brakes half open,"* Berlucki said. *"Gears down and locked."*

*"Hope they shooed those alligators off the runway."*

It looked slightly different to me, because they were landing at Cape Canaveral. Most of the shuttle landings I'd seen before had been at Edwards. One had been at White Sands in New Mexico.

"Way to go, Poleskis," I cheered. "Grease her down good. You made that runway look like it was made of Teflon."

Atlantis had braked to a stop. Support vehicles were racing towards it. A textbook landing.

Cholo leaned back.

"Critical mass has got me stumped," he said, "but our primordial is below it, whatever it is. It didn't suck the earth in. Just ate most of its molten core. We've got a hollow earth now."

He got off the Internet and maximized the math display.

"Black hole did that?" I asked.

"Yeah, well, according to the parameters I chose."

He took off his glasses and wiped them with a bit of tissue paper. His eyes, just as I remembered, always became momentarily unfocused when his glasses came off.

"Arbitrary parameters, of course," I said.

"Reasonable ones."

"So the black hole eats up the earth's core. And that's how it makes its point."

"Something like that. It's a worm inside an apple."

# XIII

It was midnight black all day. It was raining stars, and it was going to shower meteors.

The black hole sat.

In geosynchronous orbit.

# Close to the Bone

Somewhere in the hills. In the South. Behind Argao and Dalaguete. With the farmer. Farmer and son.

Chinggoy's been here before. When he was nine. Now it's different. He's an adult now. In between jobs. His father's given him a choice. Drug rehab center or a vacation with the *sa-op* in the badlands. Chinggoy's opted for the rustic spell.

The farmer's land is a pittance. Adjoins the elder Echevarría's hectares. Grows corn and coconuts. For both himself and his *agawon*. A marginal existence. Scratching a living out of the flinty soil. Chinggoy sees it now with the eye of an outsider, sees the parched earth. Sees it slowly cracking in the summer heat. The farmer is his father's vassal. His father is the liege lord. The land is still in feudal times. He doesn't care. Life here is lived close to the bone. Always has been. That's all there is to it.

Botyok returns at dusk, *buyot* clinking. Bamboo jug of palm wine hanging by its handle from his shoulder. Empties the bag: bottles of beer. Still cold. For the city boy.

Chinggoy bristles at the implicit reverse snobbery. But then again, Botyok's just being considerate. Not all city boys know how to drink *tubâ*.

Botyok is short for Francisco.

The farmer is Manoy Panyong.

Chinggoy feels awkward using the Visayan honorific. He still calls the farmer Tatay. First called him that when he and Botyok were kids, fast playmates. Better that way. Makes the farmer feel he has two sons. Or Chinggoy two fathers.

The man's a widower. Wife died four, five years back, Chinggoy seems to recall. Can't even remember her name. It's on the tip of his tongue. He recalls the farmer's name now, Epifanio. Epifanio Bukiron. Panyong for short.

Chinggoy drinks the beer. The sky is clearer here, the stars brighter. Botyok offers his father a bottle. The farmer shakes his head. "Not used to *cerveza*," he mutters. Use of the plural shows politeness, but there's that undertone. Contempt, it sounds like. Accepts a glass of *tubâ*. Quaffs it in one go.

Stilted conversation. Farmer and son speak the Visayan language the Southern way. Funny drawl, no contractions. The difference in accent is a function of distance. Emphasizes how far from home Chinggoy is. Gives him a sense of freedom. But his Visayan doesn't jibe too well with theirs. City-slick and street smart, it probably jars their ears. Good thing they're all untalkative. The farmer's one of those strong silent types. Chinggoy's a quiet guy. Botyok is taciturn.

The last bottle is warm by the time Chinggoy gets to it. He drinks it slowly. The stars seem timeless. When the beer's all gone the farmer passes him the glass. Chinggoy drinks. After that round, he knows he can't leave the jug unfinished. So passes the evening. Chinggoy passes out.

Daytimes Chinggoy lolls around. The farmer's away most of the time. Out in the fields. Botyok, too. Noontimes Botyok comes home, cooks lunch. Brings his father's portion over to the fields.

Chinggoy reads. He's brought a few paperbacks along. Listens to music. His Sony Discman is a curiosity here. He's noted Botyok staring at it. And at his CD's. Botyok wants it, he knows. Wants to borrow the thing. Go around wearing the earphones like a woman's headband. Only, he's too shy to ask. Chinggoy leaves it lying around sometimes. When he goes off for a walk. Wouldn't mind if Botyok used it for a short while. But when he gets back it's always untouched.

Chinggoy takes the walks when the heat becomes tolerable, in the afternoon. Sometimes he sees a man in the distance. Or a knot of men. Sometimes they pass each other. They always greet him. He'll nod, or return the greeting. They seem to know whose son he is. They're scruffy men, farmers by the look of them, people from around these parts. Once, out later than usual, nightfall catches him still abroad. Seeing a light, he goes to take a look. It's a camp, men around a fire. Cooking supper. He crouches, keeps out of sight. A band of them, guns within easy reach. A few M-16's. At least one AK-47.

More often Chinggoy gets home at dusk, two hours or so after setting out. By then Botyok's climbed a coconut tree and brought down a few young nuts. Chinggoy's glad of this superb treat, tender coconut meat in its own milk, after his walks.

He's asked Botyok about these people he's seen.

"Mostly from around here," Botyok says. "A few new faces."

"Some of them are armed."

"Must be the Baho'g Ilok Gang. They were here once, Kumander Pongkol and the rest of them. Tatay talked to them. Told me to go away. They drank *tubâ*. Afterwards I asked about it. He said it was nothing."

Baho'g Ilok Gang. Mixing up Visayan and English words, in the modern guerrilla way. Smelly Armpits Gang. The coarser the name, the better.

Chinggoy's got something else on his mind. He's told Botyok about it, what he's looking for. He asks about it again.

"Cotton?" Botyok repeats. Can't understand it. Why would anyone look for cotton here?

"Wild cotton," Chinggoy says again. "Growing wild. Somewhere."

"*Doldol?*" Botyok asks. "There's a tree over there. I'll show you."

Doldol is kapok. *Ceiba pentandra*. Entirely different. Cotton is of the *Gossypium* family.

"No, not doldol," Chinggoy says. "*Gapas*. Cotton."

"Well, nothing like that here," Botyok concludes. "We can buy it in town, though. Absorbent. Or buds. You know, Q-tips."


Chinggoy's convinced there must be a shrub or two around someplace. He only has to look for it. He's got the time. Summer wears on. Now and then the sky shows a wisp of cirrus very high up, never a hope of rain. The heat is enervating. Chinggoy bathes in the creek twice a day. Morning and evening.

One day Botyok asks if he'd like to go with him to town. Time to buy supplies. Matches, canned sardines, kerosene. Chinggoy goes. Dalaguete. Botyok calls it Dalagit. The Spanish spelling is vestigial, a syllable too long.

On the way back Botyok takes a shortcut. He points to a shrub in someone's yard.

"There's your cotton," he says.

Chinggoy stops to talk to the housewife puttering in the garden. He asks her what the plant is called.

"*Gapas sanglay*," she says. Chinese cotton.

Chinggoy's heard of it. *Gossypium barbadense*. Or maybe *Gossypium herbaceum*, he's not sure which. Imported by Chinese traders in Spanish times. Not what he's looking for.

The woman's house is a typical *nipà* hut. Raised from the ground as if on stilts. There's usually a pig or some chickens in the space under it. Here it's got a contraption he's never seen before.

"What's that?" he asks, pointing to it.

"Oh, it's an old loom. My grandmother used to weave cloth on it. It was her mother's before that."

"What cloth?"

"Cotton. From plants like this. My *lola* used to say the other kind was better, the plant she called *gapas tu-od*."

Real cotton. The old Visayan words somehow imply that other cottons aren't quite the real thing. Chinggoy asks:

"What about that *gapas tu-od*?"

"Well, nobody grew it anymore. And nobody uses these things anymore. There was just no money in it."

When they get back the farmer tells them he has to go to town. Unlocks the tool shed. Whips off an old blanket. *Voilà*, a trail bike. Blue Yamaha DT 125. None the worse for wear.

"Got it secondhand," Manoy Panyong says, waving away inquiries. "On installment."

He's off in a cloud of dust. Chinggoy's mind won't deal with how the farmer financed this acquisition. No matter.

There's still time for his walk. The search is still on. Finding the wrong species doesn't disappoint him. Rather, it bolsters the idea. That cotton can indeed grow here. He's heard something of the sort. When a cousin of his father's was at the house. Years ago. His own namesake, Ramón. Tio Monching, his father happened to mention later, had written a paper. On cotton. In the South. Was planning to publish it. Limited edition.

All too soon it's time to head home. Shortest way is through the cornfields. Got to be careful. Corn leaves are razor-edged. In the center of the field are weeds growing in between the rows of cornstalks. He goes on. Careless farmer. Can't weed his fields right. It must affect his harvest. More of the weeds further on. He looks at one. He's seen these serrated leaves before. Of course, *Cannabis sativa*. Growing lush. Full of THC. He wonders how it's related to rice, *Oryza sativa*. He picks a few leaves.

Not far from the house he finds a place to dry the leaves in the sun.

The next day he goes to town, Alcoy this time, to buy rolling paper. None to be found. He settles for a few sheets of onionskin paper.

He browses in the town library and comes across a thin book. *Rediscovery in Southern Cebu*, by Ramón Echevarría. Cebu City, 1974. So Tio Monching had got that paper published, after all. Is the author still alive? Hasn't heard of him in years. Must be sixtyish now. This uncle's from a Manila branch of the family. Lived a few years in Cebu. When his job took him south.

Chinggoy skims through the book. Very well written. The author is a learned man. Quotes from Pigafetta and Chao Ju Kua. Disputes Rizal's assertion that Chao's "Ma-yi" was Mindoro. Echevarría argues that Ma-yi was Cebu. The argument is brilliant, persuasive, logical. Chinggoy can't follow it. The book bores him.

He climbs a mango tree. Lazes around up there in the branches. Discman on his belt. Good thing he brought a lot of spare batteries, Energizers. Earphones turn his head into an echo chamber. The old Rolling Stones. Steely Dan, Supertramp, U2. Sting. Nirvana, Joey Ayala, Talking Heads. Judas Priest. The old Mahavishnu Orchestra. He's got eclectic tastes. He sees Botyok leading the carabao to the tree. Mud pool near the bole, in the shade. The animal knows it, rushes for the pool. Sinks into the mud. Grunts in contentment. Reminds Chinggoy of the time he and Botyok played tag in the branches of this very mango tree. Nine-year-old brats, both of them. Had so much fun they forgot about the carabao's cooling-off wallow. The animal overheated, ran amok. Tore through the cornfields. Cut quite a swath. Manoy Panyong hard put to recapture the beast. After he got it into the mud pool, he went for them. Gave them a good whacking. The memory of it causes a twinge of pain in Chinggoy's rump.

"*Agaray, 'Tay!*" Botyok is yelling again, "*Ayaw na, 'Tay!*"

He is yelling, too.

"*Agay, 'Tay!*"

But it was such a long time ago. He's grown up now. So has Botyok.

Botyok looks up, sees him. Hoists himself up the tree to join him.

Chinggoy lets the tune finish, then passes him the Discman.

Botyok slips the earphones on. Turns the volume up. Chinggoy can hear the music escaping from the earphones. Then Botyok surprises him. Botyok sings along.

*It's the ho-wo-oh-wo-ong-ky tonk women*

*Gimme, gimme, gimme the honky tonk blues!*

After a few days, the leaves seem dry enough. Chinggoy wraps them up in the onionskins, stuffs the wad into a pouch. Later he'll tear off a bit of onionskin, crumble a leaf into it, and roll a joint. Mactan stone it's not, but Argao gold's reputation is as good as Baguio gold's. Or Maui wowie's. Or even Colombian dope's. Second to none, the way it hits. Psychoactive ingredient, he remembers now, is delta-9-tetrahydrocannabinol. THC for short. Cripes, his mind must be warped, rattles off all these crazy things. His only regret is these plants weren't grown in ultraviolet light. That'd have converted most of the inert cannabinoids into one-delta isomers. For one hell of a real good *expanded* blow.

Saturday again. Beer and palm wine again. Chinggoy sticks to beer. As the night deepens, *tubâ* loosens the farmer's tongue.

"Titing Kulas and me, childhood playmates," he says.

"Titing Kulas?" Chinggoy queries Botyok.

"Kumander Pongkol."

"Good man. Very good. Helped me rush Liliang to the hospital when she got the dengué. Took care of the hospital. Doctor, private nurse, medicines. Found blood donors. From among his men, I think. Then he shouldered the funeral expenses. Has never asked me to pay him back. Payable when able, is all he said. Good man. *Siempre*, good tax collector, too. Progressive taxes. Ha ha!"

"What about the motorcycle?" Chinggoy asks. He means to probe into its financing.

"Just the thing for these hills," the farmer says. Dismissing the subject. "Now, Botyok here, I've been telling him to find a girl. If he wants, I'll find one for him. Time he got married. I want grandchildren."

"No, Tatay," Botyok protests, "I don't want a wife. There's nothing like being single."

Chinggoy goes off to relieve himself. Father and son are getting into a heated debate. He rolls a joint, quickly smokes it. Behind a tree. Only a stone's throw from them. But downwind.

Rejoining them, he pretends to listen. It's hitting him good now. Boosting him to full alpha state. He whistles half-tunelessly. Then the lyrics burst out from the recesses of his memory. In a rush. He breaks into song. Startling the farmer and Botyok.

*I have climbed*

*the highest mountain*

*I have sailed*

*across the sea*

*Only to be with you,*

*only to be with you*

*But I still*

*haven't found*

*What I'm looking for*

He closes his eyes a moment. He's in another time, another age. Cotton grows all over the place. The Visayans weave it into cloth. *Lumpot*, they call it. Take it to Sugbu, barter for it with the Sanglay, the Chinese. For metal implements. Knives, needles. Porcelain and celadon ware. The Sanglay come in their batwinged junks with the onset of the northeast monsoon, the *amihan*. They stay the summer, going around the three islands, the *San-si*. Sugbu, Bo-ol, and the land of the Hay-tan. It's for the Hay-tan or Agtà that the Spanish, centuries later, name that island Negros. The Sanglay leave with the *habagat*, the southwest wind. The Sanglay know the secret of weaving silk. Are proud of it. Disdain the cultivation of cotton. It's the Indians who grow and weave cotton. This art they've passed on to the Visayans. Via the old empire of the Sri Vijayâ. It was a remnant of the latter that founded Sugbu. Between two rivers. Facing the island of the Mat-an.

The Sanglay need a good cheap cloth for the masses. They find it in Ma-yi. An island lying northeast to southwest, ten days' sail north of Po-ni or Borneo. Chao Ju Kua writes that the cloth is called *yu-ta*. Not a Chinese word.

It's a borrowed Visayan word, *yutà*. Soil. Or earth. For the cloth that comes straight out of the land. The Sanglay trade for it, and for gold, beeswax and civet cats, with the best of their glazed porcelains. The trade begins during the T'ang Dynasty, and goes on through the Sung, Ming and Yüan Dynasties. The South grows prosperous on cotton. Its people take exquisite pottery to their graves, for use in the afterworld.

The Spanish arrive, change everything. All trade between Manila and Acapulco only, on the annual galleon. The cotton growers of the South are deprived of their traditional market. Cotton becomes a loser. *Lumpot* has to compete with *medriñaque,* and it doesn't do too well. The Visayans are given a new crop, *maize* from Nueva España. They take to the Mexican plant, having no choice. Corn has shallow roots, and a few centuries of it depletes and erodes the soil. Gives the farmer poorer and poorer harvests down the generations. The mountains of the South are bald now, the backbone of the island exposed. Now the Southerner lives hand to mouth. Times are lean. Have been for ages. Life is mean. Always, close to the bone.

"Go to bed, Tsinggoy," the farmer is shaking him, "you've fallen asleep right there."

Up in the mango tree again. Relaxes in his favorite spot, where the branches fork. Reclines in languor. Turns on the Discman. The Allman Brothers Band. Duane Allman is still alive, still giving the band the longhaired sound of his lead guitar. Died a long time ago in a motorcycle crash, but for Chinggoy the music lives on.

Botyok arrives, leading the carabao. He's got a sprig in his hand.

The beast in the mud, Botyok climbs up and hands over the broken-off branch. Leaves, buds, flowers, bolls. All there. Chinggoy unravels a bit of cotton, estimates the staple.

"Where did you find this?"

"Not too far from here. I'll take you there. When I've put the carabao away."

"Very long staple. It would weave into a cloth of high quality. Better than the other one, that *gapas sanglay*."

"We walked past this shrub once, Tatay and me. A long time ago. Nanay was still alive then. He pointed at it and said it was *gapas tu-od*. I remembered it only now."

"Good thing you remembered at all."

Chinggoy takes out a joot, lights up.

"Wow, so he is an **adok-adok**." Botyok says. Knows a bit of city slang.

Chinggoy passes the jay. Botyok shakes his head, but his hand reaches out for the toke.

Two puffs, then he's coughing. Tears come to his eyes.

Chinggoy feels it hitting him right away. He puts a Bob Marley CD in and hands the Discman to Botyok. Botyok dances the reggae, balancing on a thick branch, with exaggerated movements. They're laughing themselves silly.

"My name not Botyok," Botyok says. "My name Botvinnik!"

He falls. Grabs a thin branch on the way down, lands on his feet. Chinggoy jumps down after him. Only a six-foot drop.

Chinggoy lights up again. More ganja. They're bent over it, snorting smoke, when they hear someone coming. From the direction opposite the house. It's Manoy Panyong.

*"Adis-adis, ha?"*

He finds two sticks and starts beating them up.

"Bad influence," he huffs as he whacks Chinggoy.

*"Leche 'ng yawâ,"* as he canes Botyok.

Both of them howling all the while. The farmer's putting his back into his strokes, and the pain is excruciating.

*"Aguroy, 'Tay!"* they scream, powerless before the father's righteous wrath.

*"Ayaw na, 'Tay!"*

# Du-awon, Backcover Blurbs for a Volume on

"Du-awon is the antithesis of all those places you can't miss. It's a sure miss. The turnoff is unmarked except for a crude handlettered sign, tacked so high up a coconut tree no one ever sees it. It's as if it was meant to be underlooked."

—Boots

"Even if you know where it is, it takes an effort of will to leave the smooth Marigondon road. You've rounded the last curve, topped the last rise, and can smell the beaches dead ahead. You're on the homestretch now, all straight and downhill, so you step on the gas and accelerate. Then Du-awon pops up like a stray thought from the back of your mind, and before you know it you're standing on your brakes and pulling the car into that tight, hundred-and-twenty-degree left turn. A sense of guilt creeps over you, too, as you drag the car by its ass a full mile over that rough, winding, God-forsaken rocky road."

—Yitschak

"He who hesitates before he dives is chicken. He who swims in kneedeep water should use a bucket. If you can't do even that but still can picnic, bring chicken in a bucket."

—Spike

"Du-awon Beach is no beach. I kid you not. Du-awon is all cliffs, rocks, drowndeep water, and coves quiet as ponds. Frog-man jumps in: watersmack."

—Eric

# Notes from Underwater

From our clifftop to the brine was a sheer twelve feet and then, the tide on the surge, a depth of twenty-four. Full fathom four. Spike and I were laughing ourselves silly doing platform dives. The swan dive was all we knew, but neither of us was about to admit it. We were going for the jacknife, the pike, the back dive, the half-gainer—and turning out ignominious flops.

Spike, a Manila cousin of mine, often came to Cebu on field assignment. A few days' work, a few evenings in Cebu City's sleaziest nightspots, and he would be primed for a Sunday at a Mactan beach. We always went to Du-awon. For both of us, the only way to get into the sea was headfirst. We would shudder at the mere mention of some other beach where fine white sands gently sloped into emerald waters. It was unthinkable to wade into the sea. Only waddling ducks and quack doctors went into the water *feetfirst*.

A banca was coming our way. The two sunscorched wizened men paddling it contrasted with their passenger at the bow. In a swimsuit of shimmering colors, she wore a widebrimmed straw hat, snobbish sunglasses, and a Coral Reef Hotel towel around her shoulders.

Spike and I looked at each other, then burst out laughing. We knew what we were going to do. The impulse grabbed both of us at the same time. We leaped off the cliff together, at the precise moment when the banca was closest. We spread our wings out in a dual swan dive, laughing like crazy. We made a double splash that must have seemed as one. When we came up we were still laughing, the girl had whipped her glasses off to look us in the eye, and she was indeed very beautiful.

Vicente "Boots" Bandillo laughed when I told him about that dive. He didn't think guys like us rated so much as a passing glance from a pretty girl. And it was of course absolutely impossible to jump in laughing and come up still laughing.

I mumbled something about the mammalian diving reflex.

"Aw, come on," Boots said, "don't give me that."

I got up and stepped out on the edge. I took a deep breath and then did a swan dive, just to show him. Boots was Cebu's foremost poet as far as I could tell (an assertion only Mel Baclay would dispute) but his flights were strictly on paper. He couldn't fly off a cliff like I could. He could only fly off the handle, which he did whenever a literary quorum was attained.

I swam back to the cliffside, climbed the bamboo ladder, and returned to the rented hut. The bottle of rum was half finished. I poured a tot and, for form's sake, engaged Boots in a literary dispute. Boots couldn't abide drinking companions who weren't all-around arguers.

"You really ought to try a little punctuation, Boots," I said. "Just because Merwin and Strand don't doesn't mean you shouldn't, too. You're missing a lot. Shades of meaning. Nuances. Inflections."

"Well, at least I don't write stale, effete prose," Boots shot back. "Why, too many of your sentences end with prepositions. Too many of them have dangling infinitives. Hell, if you were in my grammar class, you wouldn't pass. You'd fail the course, and fail miserably."

"Your poems are utterly bereft of social relevance."

"Your stories are totally devoid of imagination and craft."

It was a pleasant way to pass the afternoon, drink inflaming the invective, sun setting a path of liquid fire on the sea below. A beam of sunlight came out a mini-rainbow after passing through the glass Boots had been drinking out of from.

"What was it again that Krip Yuson said to you?"

I loved kidding Boots about that. Shortly after Alfred A. Yuson published *Sea Serpent*, his first book of poetry, Boots wrote a scathing review of it in an obscure magazine called *Little Finger*. Boots said things like "Apparently Yuson's memory tongues itself, then is merely exhausted." Since *Little Finger* had a circulation of 500, mostly in Cebu and Davao, he figured he was safe. A copy, however, somehow reached Yuson. The next month Yuson came to Cebu for a poetry reading session. Boots was there, of course. When Jun Dumdum slyly but formally introduced them to each other, Yuson took one sardonic look at Boots. "*Ang bata mo pala*," he said. Just that one short line, and so much for Boots's career as a critic!

"Oh, Krip didn't say anything much," Boots said, shaking his head.

I downed my shot, disdained the chaser, went out and dove into the Hilutungan Channel. I breaststroked underwater, broke the surface and switched to an overarm stroke, then struck out for Olanggo Island.

A mask and snorkel popped up, then a hand giving me the finger. It was Yitschak. I dirtyfingered right back. He passed me his spare mask and snorkel, and went back to breathing from his tank. I managed to get the gear on while treading water. His name was Isaac Fischbein, he

hailed from Boston, Massachusetts, we had been neighbors for a few months, and I had taken to calling him
Yitzhak. He corrected my pronunciation until I could say
"Yitschak" with a Yiddish accent. "Yeah," he said when I
got it right, "that's the way the rabbi at my synagogue says
it. Could be why I stopped going there." He motioned me
down to the bottom. Near the seafloor, in five-fathom water,
he pointed out a group of three or four fish hovering above
a bit of coral. Brightly colored, their ornate pectoral fins
fanned slowly back and forth, like angels' wings. He poked
at the nearest one without quite touching it, and the fish
reared back. I exhaled a stream of bubbles and Yitschak
passed me his mouthpiece. The air from his tank was cool
and crisp. Going up, we took turns breathing, passing the
mouthpiece back and forth. We broke through and trod
water.

"Scorpionfish," he said. "Poisonous, but they keep their
cool. Just don't provoke them."

He slid back underwater. I stayed on the surface,
breathing through the snorkel, and swam out to the ledge.
The trench there afforded a sudden drop of 130 feet. He
sank into the blue-green depths, his blond hair as bright as
the orange and blue of the anemones and coral. His outsize flippers made him look like some monster frog. The
spear gun held at the ready and the knife strapped to his
shin gave him a touch of Rambo. He looked up and signalled me, tip of right index finger hanging on to the circle
formed by his left thumb and forefinger. It meant either
"Hang on to your ass" or "Am hanging on by the ass"; I
wasn't sure which. I signalled back, rubbing my two middle
fingers in a cross, the aquatic equivalent of the stage actor's
"Break a leg." Then I turned back and slowly returned to
the cliffs of Du-awon.

None of those three guys knew each other. I suppose they were in Du-awon on three different occasions. My memory is no help. Never good at faces, unreliable with chronologies, all my memory will begrudge is an inventory of what slight changes time hath wrought on Du-awon. Here the bamboo ladder for climbing back up the cliff after a dive has rusted away into metal. The circular huts have been squared, like algebraic symbols, and are thatched now with *nipa* which must have grown right there on the roof, pushing off the *cogon*.

My memory brings back the monitor lizard I startled one morning, among the rocks. It scuttled away and fled into the brush beside a swampy inner cove. I stopped a moment and wondered what else might be lurking there, what creatures essentially unchanged since the dawn of creation still held out in Du-awon.

Spike, too, loved Du-awon's prehistoric ambience. There was of course something atavistic about the guy himself, as could be inferred from the mere fact that he preferred his nickname to his real name. His official name was Ian Rossanno. It didn't go too well with his surname, Kapauan. So he always went by the monicker Spike Kapauan.

That surname came from the Hiligaynon name of a tree related to the *narra* and the *laua-an*. The wood of the *kapaw-an* burned very slowly. In the olden days, before they had matches, Spike's Ilonggo ancestors would leave a hunk of *kapaw-an* smoldering in the fireplace overnight. In the morning it would still be glowing, and they could start a new blaze from its embers. Spike struck me as a guy who kept stoking his secret inner fires, and I always felt the urge to douse him with cold water. He had recently read James Michener's novel *Centennial*, and now he hastened to put Du-awon in proper geological context.

Du-awon first belonged to the sea, Spike said, and had only lately become part of the land. Some 300 million years ago there was only one landmass, the continent of Pangæa, and one ocean, the Sea of Tethys. Mactan had not yet been formed from the basalt of the seafloor. There was no Cebu, indeed no Philippine archipelago. Eons went by. Pangæa broke up into uneven halves between 180 and 130 million years ago. The half called Laurasia proceeded to break up further, into Asia, Europe and North America. The other half, Gondwana, split up into Africa, Antarctica and South America. None of these bore the soil that would become Mactan. Mactan came from no continent; it was a gift of the sea.

"Which part became Atlantis?" I asked. "And Lemuria? And Mu?"

"Oh, some of those," Spike said. "I'm not really sure."

He glugged down beer, exhaled, then took a deep breath. He meant to continue. North America left Eurasia, a part of it splitting off into Greenland, and went to join South America. Africa hit Eurasia and part of the former tore off and stuck to the latter as Arabia. Antarctica lost great chunks that became Australia and India. The subcontinent of India set a speed record, 70 million years ago, when it left Antarctica. A piece of it lagged behind as Madagascar, but it took the sprinting India a mere 40 million years to crash into Asia. The impact was so great it sent land thrusting up as the Himalayan mountains. In fact, Spike told me, India is still underthrusting into Asia at about five centimeters a year. It was probably this collision that set in motion the forces that pushed Mactan up from the sea.

I had lost the line of reasoning but Spike went on. He was gung-ho on plate tectonics. He was also on his sixth beer. I was on my second. I opened two bottles, both for me. I would catch up.

"The earth's crust is composed of about twenty lithospheric plates," Spike said. "They ride on top of the asthenosphere, which is molten for the most part. When a plate made of continental rock subducts into another plate made of seafloor basalt, volcanic islands rise. These islands are fed by magma from below. This was how the Philippine archipelago came into being. When the Indo-Australian plate subducted into the Eurasian plate, pushing up the Himalayas, the Pacific plate was also moving in from the east. Caught in between was the tiny Philippine plate. The pressure caused seamounts to rise and become islands."

"What's a seamount?"

"O, *chong*, isn't it obvious? It's an underwater mountain."

"Kindly continue, my dear esteemed cousin, *changna mo*."

"Erosion has played its part, too. This part of Mactan's coast, facing the waves, has been ground to sand over a few million years. That's why all the beach resorts are here. Du-awon has another few million years before its rocks, too, get ground into sand. It's been putting up a stout resistance."

He was right of course, at least about Mactan having once been the bottom of a sea. I had done enough digging in the soil of Mactan to know it was full of rocks with fossils in them. Clams mainly, and coral. Never fossils of land animals. No dinosaurs or mastodons. Since the fos-

silized clamshells always looked like the discards from some
recent meal, I guessed the rocks were not very ancient.

I asked Spike which era it was when Mactan rose from
the sea.

"Cenozoic," he said. "Probably the late quaternary period."

"Not Ordovician or Silurian? From the Paleozoic? After all, there are fossil clams in these rocks."

"We haven't carbon-dated them. They're probably recent. But do you know what a better indicator of newness
is? No? It's the number of species of freshwater fish and
anurans. I don't remember the figures for the fish, but I
seem to recall that Mactan has about 15 species of frogs
and toads. That's the number of species in the Visayas
region generally. There are about 85 species of frogs and
toads in Borneo. Only 15 have made it here. On the island
of Luzon, there are only seven species. Fewer land bridges
to there from Borneo."

"You haven't been here during the rainy season. When
the fields are flooded, the voice of the anuran is heard all
over the land. It always sounds like a million different species."

Spike laughed, but he didn't comment on that.

An airliner did a wide turn overhead, lowering its landing gear as we watched.

"You know, I saw Mactan from the plane," Spike said,
"while we were still over Cebu. All those bald mountains.
Mactan looks good from a distance. It's the twin runways
that stand out. They make the island look like an aircraft
carrier."

I didn't bother to correct him. There was only one runway; the twin was actually a taxiway. I knew what he meant. I'd been to Manila the month before, and had also seen Mactan from the air on the flight home. The twin runways subtended a slight angle to the axis indicated by Punta Engaño, exactly the angle of those canted flight decks on the nuclear leviathans.

I guessed that Spike's plane had made a straight-in approach. Mine had gone by the book into a landing pattern, going downwind and on into a full circle before coming into the wind on final approach. This gave me a chance to eyeball the beaches on Mactan's east coast. I strained my eyes looking for Du-awon. I nearly missed it. At the last moment, before it left the field of view my window allowed me, I saw it. Craning my neck, I drank in the surreal outlines of the rocky cliffs, lovingly counted all five of its coves.

On the other beaches, which were strips of white sand, the waves broke evenly, in regular patterns. On Du-awon there was a difference. The waves would break at the leading edges of the rocks, then curve in to sweep into the coves. The rebounds from the cliffs and the coves were out of sync, and churned up a mess of foam.

Du-awon from the air resembled a giant paw, as if the five coves had been clawed off by fingers and thumb. Something had held on to Mactan as it rose from the sea, and Du-awon was where it had lost its grip. It hadn't given up easily. Huge ragged chunks of rock had been torn off in the struggle.

I wondered where the other paw had grabbed and it came to me in a flash: at Gu-wanon, where else? Gu-wanon was on the other side of Mactan. A cove facing Mandaue, with the Bridge visible a couple of kilometers to the south.

An underground stream had its outlet at Gu-wanon. It kept
the cove clean despite the pollution in the Mactan Channel. The outlet could be seen only at low tide, being underwater at high tide. It gave the cove its name. Gu-wanon
meant "the place where it comes out," from the root *guwà*,
"to come out."

Gu-wanon, or at least the foreshore rights to it, was
owned by Dr. Tony Alcantara, a Mactan physician who
once spent half a decade in Boston, practicing his profession where the patients paid top dollar. In Boston he had
once treated Isaac Fischbein for a minor ailment. We ran
into him one evening at a rock concert at the Lapulapu
City tennis courts. Yitschak recalled Dr. Tony quite well.
It was the doctor who couldn't remember Fischbein. He
had to grope for the name. "Feinstein, isn't it? Or is it
Lowenstein?"

"Fischbein," Yitschak said. "Small world. What's up,
doc?"

Yitschak became my neighbor when he moved out of
the Heidelberg Pension near the Bridge and rented a house.
The house next to mine had just become vacant. I watched
the tall foreigner move in with his Filipina girlfriend. His
hair and beard were blond and his eyes very blue. I was
sure he was a German, because he always went around in
short pants. Americans were clean-shaven and wore ties,
or were scrappy and wore denims. Either way they nodded their heads all the time, and gestured with their loose
limbs in awkward ways. It was the Italians who had eloquent hands, and the French too. I could always tell the
latter by their Gallic shrugs, and their meaningless but
useful expression "Shpuh!", always said with palms turned
up. As for the Germans, they zipped around on dirt bikes

and had magic right hands. The moment a German's right hand was free, a bottle of beer miraculously grew out of it.

Fischbein however turned out to be a Yankee. That first afternoon he and his girlfriend were just sitting around, so I invited him over for a beer. Born in Boulder, Colorado. Lived in Boston, in Lexington where the American Revolution started off, until he was 17. Lived alone in California four years, got a degree in Mechanical Engineering at Stanford. Went back to Boston and worked for Airflow Dynamics, a company that made fans and volutes on subcontract for automobile engines. Most of the cars made in Detroit couldn't run without his company's products.

"Ever fight in Vietnam?"

"Nah, I was too young for 'Nam. I was born in 1964."

He didn't have the vaunted Boston accent. The years in the West must have erased it, if he ever had it. He was so taciturn he should have been from Vermont. He didn't confide things easily. He fretted about Cheryl. She didn't go out of the house much and sometimes she got kind of manic-depressive. He wanted to marry her. Her Filipino husband had left her some years before but there'd been no divorce, not even a legal separation, so she wasn't free to marry again. The priest had said so. The lawyer had said pretty much the same thing. Cheryl couldn't become Mrs. Fischbein, not for any amount of *chutzpah*. His name was a dead giveaway. Jewish, wasn't it? Yeah, sure. Shit, man, for crying out loud, why not say it—yes, he was a fucking Jew. No hooked nose, no earlocks, but his beard could vie with any prophet's, and he did have a circumcised cock. "Sometimes I think with my *oh-ten*," he said.

I didn't know what to say to that. The Visayan word, coming out as it did in that American accent, hadn't sounded obscene. Just the same, it took me by surprise.

His father, Nathan Fischbein, was one of the few remarkable Jews who lasted out World War II in Berlin. Living in hiding, like Anne Frank, you know? Only, Anne Frank's family had hidden out in Amsterdam. Nathan Fischbein hid underground, like a mole, in the very capital of Nazi Germany, in Berlin itself. In a cellar. Cleverly concealed trapdoor. Loyal friends passing him food. And so forth and so on. Six years living blind, 1939 through 1945, so that afterwards his craving for sunlight became an obsession. Did I know how many Jews survived World War II in Berlin? I had no idea. Maybe 1,500, he said. Out of some 6,000. It took a lot to ferret them out, raid them up and kill them off. Some were betrayed. Many starved. Some got hit by Allied bombs.

Nathan Fischbein moved to Palestine in 1947, running the British blockade. He lived in a kibbutz and danced like the young King David when the State of Israel was founded in 1948. In 1954 he married a Jewish-American girl who had come home to Zion in those early, idealistic years.

When they lost their daughter to the bullets of an Arab gang that staged a commando raid on their kibbutz, they decided to go to the United States. Isaac was born there. He grew up speaking his mother's English and his father's German. His parents conducted arguments in Yiddish, so he learned that, too.

Strange how, going with a foreigner, we ran into his compatriots all the time. In Du-awon we ran into an old hand named Huey. Potbellied and bald, he was from Atlanta.

"From Boston, you say?"

"Sure. Lexington, thereabouts."

"Now, Ah find that hard to believe, mistuh. You sho' doan' have no Boston accent. Y'all sound lahk a *German*. Hell, ya look lahk one, too."

I could sense Yitschak's dander going up, but he played it cool. He was as laid back as they come.

"Spent some time in California. Guess that took care of my accent."

"Hey, Boston's in Massachusetts, right? Tell me, do you know Ted Kennedy?"

Yitschak didn't hesitate.

"Hey, sure. He played shortstop for the Boston Red Sox."

"You know Tip O'Neill?"

"Guy that played guard for the Boston Celtics."

"Got one last question, mistuh. Who was JFK? That's jay...eff...kay. As in John Fitzgerald Kennedy."

Yitschak had to stop and think. He looked like he was thinking hard. The question really stumped him.

"He was President," Yitschak said at last. "President of the United States."

"Ho-kay, ya been to Boston. Heck, Ah still think you're a kraut. You're the epitome of Aryan perfection."

Yitschak conceded the point with a shrug. He'd told Huey his name was Glass, Jack Glass, and I guessed his real name would bait Huey into calling him a Zionist or, worse, a kike. Huey was the loquacious type and we let him talk. Said he'd been at 'nuther beach jes t'other week, happens it wuz low tide, and he wades out half a mile and the water's still up only to his knee. Damn if there warn't coupla guys 'nuther half-mile further out, and they wuz in only up to their neck. Which was exactly why he'd come to Du-awon this time.

Yitschak had had the same experience, the first time he and Cheryl went out for a morning of scuba diving. They chartered a tricycle in front of the Heidelberg Pension. The driver took them to the end of the smooth road, they took one of those huts, and Yitschak waded out in his scuba gear. He had to go almost a mile before he got to the ledge where he could drop off into water 130 feet deep. A few days after he told me about that, I took them to Du-awon. Yitschak took two steps from our hut and jumped off the cliff, scuba gear on. He hit the water with a loud smack from his outsize flippers. I thought his face mask would tear off but his technique was good. He had learned to scuba dive in a course the US Navy gave to its frogmen. Civilians could take it for a fee.

Yitschak came back with a fair-sized *molmol* impaled on his spear and Cheryl roasted it on a grill. He called it a "parrotfish." I told him about the seasnake that lived in these waters. It was called the *tig-walo*, Visayan for "do by eight", because its poisonous bite would do you to death in eight days.

"Yeah, I've seen it," he said. "Thin, about a foot long, with yellow and orange bands. They don't mind you if you don't come close."

"Don't they single out Jews?"

He considered that for a moment.

"Maybe they should, at that. Every other kind of snake seems to."

Something in the way a shadow fell on his face suddenly brought to mind another foreigner I had known, for a semester, in college. He was an Iranian medical student, and was very quiet for a Shiite Muslim. Like Yitschak, he avoided pork. Yitschak didn't do much on the Sabbath; the Iranian prayed five times a day every Friday. The rest of the week neither of them thought too much about religion. The Iranian's name came back to me now: Ishaq Pahmudi. It gave me a sense of satisfaction to realize that this Jew and that Muslim were both named after Isaac, son of Abraham.

When Yitschak was 12 his parents took him to Berlin. They managed to arrange a visit to the Soviet sector. They passed through Checkpoint Charlie and went to the cellar Nathan Fischbein had lived in. The house over it was new; the old building had been reduced to rubble in 1945.

*"Berlin hat verstanden,"* Nathan Fischbein solemnly intoned, *"und so habe ich."*

Yitschak knew it was a saying often uttered by Berliners in the postwar years: "Berlin is still standing, and so am I."

Yitschak tried to imagine living in that dank place for six years. Fungi would grow on his skin; his hair would turn dull brown, the color of mushrooms. It occurred to him that he would be 18 when he got out, and that overwhelmed him. Thereafter it became apparent he had inherited, by some quirk of genetics, his father's passion for sunlight.

California. Hawaii. Penang. Bali. Phuket. Manado. Flying back to the US, he met Cheryl during a stopover in Seoul. He looked her up when he got back a few months later. She waited for him in Manila. Cebu the next day.

Tandag in two days, since that was when the next flight was, the place being too small to rate a daily flight. Her village, he ascertained, was inland. No prospect of swimming there. But they were still on Mactan, whose twin runways reminded him of the *Bon Homme Richard*, which he had once seen coming into San Diego. Lots of good beaches right here on Mactan, weren't there? So they stayed, deferring Tandag. Subsequently, the state of some of the beaches at low tide would probably have exasperated him. Yitschak might have gone on to Palawan if I hadn't taken them to Du-awon.

"Somebody told me," Cheryl said, "there have been several drownings here."

"Yes," I acknowledged. "Every other year or so. Once three girls, triplets, all drowned together."

"This is no place for mediocre swimmers," Yitschak said.

"Actually," I said, "It's often the strong swimmers who drown."

"Damn right," Yitschak said. "They get overconfident. Then they find themselves in straits bad swimmers never get into."

Drowning, some aspects of it, was on my mind the day Boots Bandillo took Eric Gamalinda to Du-awon. He'd called me up the day before, inviting me to join them there; Eric would like to meet me, Boots said. Well, I wanted to meet Gamalinda, too. I'd been reading his poems, stories and music reviews in various papers and magazines for some time. All the way back to the years when he still used his full resonant name, Mario Eric T. Gamalinda. I even knew that the T. stood for Trinidad. Nifty writer, that guy.

I hadn't been to Du-awon in months. My last time there I'd nearly managed to drown myself together with my nephew Tonio Dingdong. The kid was eight and had just taken the YMCA Learn to Swim course so I tossed an inflated inner tube into the Hilutungan Channel, dove in and trod water, and yelled for him to jump in and swim for the tube. Damn fool idea. He jumped in all right, he wasn't going to hedge like a sissy in front of me, but when he reached me he clung to my neck and let me do all the swimming. His weight dragged me down and I frogkicked up for a breath but he was so heavy all I got was a choking gulp of seawater so I had to hold my breath when all I wanted was to cough and when I opened my eyes underwater I saw that the current had pulled the *salvavida* downstream and I seriously doubted if I could swim fast enough underwater unable to breath, and catch up with it. Well, I did. Just barely.

Dingdong thought it was a good thrill, but didn't suggest a repeat. Nor did I offer one. And now here I was, with Boots and Eric, and Boots just had to choose the very same hut off which my nephew and I jumped off and nearly found Davy Jones's locker.

Gamalinda had recently published his first novel, *Planet Waves*. I hadn't read it. I'd been too lazy to go downtown and buy a copy. What I had last read of his was a story in the Free Press Magazine a few issues back, "Mourning and Weeping in This Valley of Tears." It was about an old woman in a coma, hanging to life by a thread, finally dying after a few weeks. Half a month after that story came out my grandmother, hale and hearty at 88, suffered a stroke and went into a coma. When I went to see her in the hospital, she was lying in bed hooked up to an array of machines. Her two daughters, my mother and my aunt, looked considerably more worn out than she did. Her breathing was quiet and regular. But when I touched her arm she did not stir, and when I spoke to her she did not rouse.

According to the doctors, my mother told me, the cerebral hemorrhage had caused irreparable brain damage. If Lola came out of the coma it would be as a vegetable. Family members came in and out of the room: uncles of mine, cousins, nieces. Everyone seemed to be observing some ancient taboo about speaking of impending death. The smallest children were told that Lola would wake up soon. Those who lived in Lola's house recalled how she had been her usual crotchety self, berating her grandchildren and spoiling her great-grandchildren. Fr. Oscar, who had officiated at most of the family's weddings and baptisms, came in and said a couple of prayers. He had administered the Anointing of the Sick the night before. I still thought the sacrament's old name, Extreme Unction, was better.

I knew my grandmother had harbored a death wish for fifteen years, ever since Lolo died. She had virtually told me so herself, if not in so many words. Lolo had died suddenly just two months short of their golden wedding anniversary. The loss hit Lola so badly that had she been a Hindu widow she would probably have committed *suttee*.

And now here she was, in a coma. Only her breathing and the rhythm of peaks and valleys on her EEG monitor indicated she was alive. Had she been capable of conscious decision I thought it likely she would have told us to quit fooling with those machines and let her go. But it was all up to her body now and only the primal instinct to cling to life was left. Her spirit might have been willing, but her flesh was too strong.

Lola had been comatose for a week when Boots Bandillo called up. I had been crossing the Mactan Channel from my place in Opon to the hospital in Mandaue but hadn't been staying overnight with Lola. I didn't want to remember her like that. To me she had always been a lively woman with a wry sense of humor and I wanted to keep it that way.

At Du-awon I nodded to Boots and shook hands with Eric Gamalinda. He struck me as a cool, laid-back, urbane Manila guy. Running to fat. I was more fit. I could still manage a swan dive or two. I wasn't sure if he knew how to swim. As for Boots, his dog paddle was so pathetic I never bothered to kid him about it.

Gamalinda's Free Press story, I wanted to tell him then and there, had bad timing. It was inauspicious, and somehow I felt it inconsiderate of him. I knew I had no right to blame him, but in some irrational way he had managed to invade my privacy and I resented it. My grandmother was confronting death and Gamalinda, employing the guise of fiction, had gussied it up and splashed it on the pages of a national magazine.

We sat there in Du-awon chatting and drinking, rum for Boots and beer for us, and I plotted revenge on Gamalinda.

Boots was asking him how heavily *Planet Waves* had been influenced by *One Hundred Years of Solitude*, the famous novel by Gabriel García Márquez. Eric admitted to being a great fan of Márquez. Boots pounced on this and said the guy's surname was García, not Márquez. In proper Spanish form the name was Gabriel García y Márquez but in Colombia they no longer bothered with the conjunction.

I hadn't read *Planet Waves* so I did a very gauche thing. I asked Eric what went on in it. I had some hopes a silly question like that would get his goat.

"Oh, it's about this guy, he sees a lot of evil in this world…"

"So then, what does he do?"

"Well, he…he turns into an angel."

I didn't know what to make of this. Weeks later, when I had read the book, I guessed that the transformation into a winged being probably had some metaphorical function. At Du-awon, however, I thought Eric was putting me on.

I plied him with drink, mustering all the corny lines I could think of.

"Here, Eric, have another. In heaven there is no beer."

"That's why we drink it here. No, thanks."

The guy was imperturbable. I went off and did a jacknife, entering the water like an arrow. I surfaced slowly, like a periscope, and watched Boots up in the hut mixing a drink in a glass. I wondered how bad it was. His mixed drinks were as bad as my metaphors.

As I was reaching for the ladder a wave caught me and I cut my finger on a sharp rock.

Dripping blood, I went past the hut to a *kamunggay* tree and broke off a branch. I stripped off the leaves from a frond in one smooth motion, crushed them into a poultice, and pressed it on my wound. The bleeding stopped.

*"Ayos pala ang malunggay,"* Eric said.

"And I thought only figs could be used for a poultice," Boots said, "like the poultice Isaiah made for Hezekiah."

"It was a paste," I said, "made by boiling the figs. It brought King Hezekiah back from the brink of death. Then Isaiah told him he would be given another fifteen years of life."

"And the amazing thing about it," Eric said, "was that the shadow made by the gnomon of the sundial went backward ten steps."

"Yes, that was amazing," I said. "Velikovsky has suggested that a sundial might move back only if the earth's rotation gets disturbed, or should I say perturbed. By a close encounter with a comet, for instance. Zecharia Sitchin says much the same thing..."

But that was not the amazing thing about it. The amazing thing was that Hezekiah had gotten fifteen more years. My grandmother had spent fifteen years waiting for death, and now she was on the brink, and I couldn't help wondering if a paste of boiled figs might snap her out of her coma.

Boots had not read Velikovsky's *Worlds in Collision* or Sitchin's *The 12th Planet* so he changed the topic.

"*Kamunggay* or *malunggay* may not be as good as fig paste," he said, "but it stopped your bleeding faster than a Band-Aid would have."

"I never knew it worked so well," Eric said. In his voice was the commercialized city dweller's awe of folk medicine.

"I wonder what this plant is called in English," Boots said. "I once had a grade-school teacher who said it's celery, but now I know better. I've eaten celery in restaurants. It's something else entirely."

"Something like *kinchay*," Eric said, "only celery has got bigger leaves."

"Maybe the English name for *kamunggay* is clubs," I said, "because what we call the *Alas sa Kamunggay* is also known as the Ace of Clubs."

"Not a valid translation," Eric laughed. "Besides, it's *Alas Kalamunggay* in Pilipino."

"Drink up, Eric," Boots said. "Us writers must drink. James Joyce couldn't write if he hadn't had a drink. Neither could Hemingway."

"No, thanks," Eric said. "I've had a lot to drink. I think I'll take a dip."

Now was my moment. I knew his sister Diana, also a writer, had drowned in 1978. I didn't know the circumstances and wasn't sure if Eric himself did. If I had heard right, she had drowned alone. But it must have left a scar on Eric's soul. They were supposed to have been particularly close. I was eager to reopen the old wound.

Eric went into the cove and waded out into chestdeep water. Boots and I went in with him, idly swishing water with our hands. I was dying to say something outrageous. I wanted to suggest that all three of us swim out as far as we could and then have...a drowning contest.

I wanted to say it in the dry, deadpan tone Melito Baclay would use. Mel had once gotten drunk with Boots and a few other Cebuano poets in the Cebu Country Club, at the lawn tables beside the swimming pool. A literary argument had flared up and Mel had lost his cool and challenged them all to a drowning contest.

I swam out into deep water, surface-dived, and came up clutching strands of seaweed I'd snatched from the bottom.

"Is it deep?" Eric asked.

"Not very," I said, resisting the impulse to say something really crazy. Then the moment had passed.

"Du-awon's so beautiful," Eric said. "I wish I could come here every weekend. What does it mean, the word 'du-awon'?"

"The root word," Boots said, is *du-aw*, 'to visit.' *Du-awon* is a verb form that should have an object. Here it doesn't, so it's dangling."

"Literally," I said, "it means 'a place to visit.' Or it could mean 'Let's visit.' Hard to tell really, since it's dangling."

"Does this place get visited by the gods?" Eric asked.

"By demons, maybe," I said. "Or by monsters. Once I saw a manta ray jump out of the water, right there. I've seen three kinds of seasnakes in these waters, the banded one whose bite kills in eight days, the long yellow one with the flattened tail, and one that's got blue bands. A really beautiful one, that blue snake. And there are monitor lizards in those rocks over there."

"Manta rays, seasnakes, monitor lizards," Boots said. "And of course killer sharks too, if you look hard enough. Would you say that all these animals might be just the prætorian guard? And that Du-awon might be one of their master's favored haunts?"

"Which master are you thinking about?" Eric asked.

"The old man of the sea himself."

"I wouldn't know about that," I said, "but whoever it is, he seems to demand tribute. The other year it was three girls, triplets. They drowned together."

"Oh God, that's awful," Eric said.

He climbed out of the water and went back to the hut. Boots went with him. I pushed off and swam out about halfway to Olanggo Island. The current took me southwest and I knew I would have to head for Tonggo Beach Resort, half a mile down the rocks from Du-awon. A cramp hit me. I reached for the affected foot to flex the toes back. I mistimed a breath and swallowed water. It made me cough, and the salty taste burned my throat. I thrashed about, fighting for a good breath, and I realized I was tiring out. All alone. Then I was hearing voices. *"Anong gimmick mo, chong?"* Spike asked. *"Hang on to your ass, man,"* said Yitschak. *"You'll fail, and fail miserably,"* Boots said. *"The sirens come out when the moon is full,"* Eric said. *"They take the moonlight in their hands and bring it back under the sea. But if one of them finds you, she'll lead you on."* I wondered if I would drown. It didn't seem too difficult. A drowning person's whole life is supposed to pass before him in one fantastic flash, but all that was on my mind was minor irritations. Goddamn that Eric for leaving the water just when the going was getting good. Goddamn that Boots. Nothing but drinking on his mind. My face went under. It would be so easy to drown. Was that a siren down there? What the hell had Eric meant, anyway? I floated just beneath the surface. I could go either way. My grandmother too hung in a shadowy netherworld. Which way would she go?

Pain shot through my cramped leg like a bolt of lightning, but my head went up for air. I found my toes and flexed them, holding my breath. I must have been turning blue when at long last I felt the pain slowly subside. And then it was gone. I went into a leisurely breaststroke and made for Tonggo.

A week later Lola slipped away, very quietly. Three weeks in a coma, just like the old woman in Gamalinda's story. The day after the funeral I bicycled to Du-awon. I rode it all the way in, over the rocky road. It would have been easier to walk, pushing the bike beside me. But no cyclist ever did that on the road to Du-awon.

I did the swan dive, the jacknife, the pike, the back dive and then, with no hesitation at all, the half-gainer. Each time, I straightened out at the right moment. And entered the water like an arrow, every time.

# Who Loves to Lie With Me

*Under the greenwood tree, who loves to lie with me*
*And tune his merrie note, unto the sweet bird's throat*
*(Come hither, come hither,*
*Here shall he see*
*No enemy*
*But winter and rough weather)*
*Who doth ambition shun, but loves to lie in the sun*
*Seeking the food he eats, and pleased with what he gets*
*(Come hither, come hither)*

—medieval English folksong

Under the mango trees, there were two ways of loll-ing around. The serious drinkers stayed on the benches, where nothing grew in the shade. The singers and guitar players soared to musical heights in the tree house. A make-shift affair, that house seemed to have grown there by it-self, a natural part of the tree. Form suited function: it was all floor plus a single wall inclined at a low angle, great for reclining against. It needed no roof under the tree's canopy of thick leaves. As for the bamboo benches, joined end to end in the shape of a tokamak encircling the bole, they were built on posts stuck into the ground. They couldn't be moved. This gave the lot of us a measure of stability, and soon we had a name. We were the Mango Boys.

Membership in the two different factions was fluid. Most of the singers drank just as heavily as the drinkers, only not as often. Conversely, the drinkers became inspired singers after the first pitcher of firewater. Being mostly tonedeaf, they usually sang offkey. They always blamed the guitar.

On a typical summer day it would begin with two guys, seeking shade, sitting on the benches. Another guy would drift in and, a critical mass having been attained, a chain reaction would be set off. Drink would appear, in a pitcher and a single glass, which would attract more guys. A guitar would materialize, prompting the gang to move up to the tree house. A real meltdown required at least two guitars. Sometimes we had as many as four.

No decent mango grove could be without a resident ghost, and ours had two. The first was the spirit of an Agtà, or Negrito aborigine, who used to wait in the branches until he could drop down on a Visayan passing underneath. In Spanish colonial times he had learned how to smoke and now was never without a cheroot of home-grown tobacco handrolled in a *lumboy* leaf. On moonless nights the telltale glow of that cigar up in the treetops might betray his presence.

The other ghost, that of a sly, treacherous woman, had been condemned to inhabit the shape of a serpent. It never came down from the trees. It might go for a whole year without eating. Then, when it had to, it would hang down by its tail from a branch, like a vine, and wait for prey.

None of us had ever actually seen these poltergeists. The glow of the cigar had been spotted a few times, though never by anyone with investigative instincts. A pig or a chicken went missing every now and then; someone always claimed he had heard its desperate squawks or deathshrieks the night before, as of an animal in the squeeze of a python's coils.

My father said his father had actually seen a chicken in the jaws of the python that was hanging by its tail from the very place our tree house now occupied. After swallowing the fowl, the snake hauled itself back up the branch and then disappeared into the innermost reaches of the tree. It happened a long, long time ago, in my grandfather's youth.

Only one person had ever seen both ghosts. This was a Japanese sniper who, sometime during World War II, had stayed up in the biggest tree for two days and nights. His intended snipee was my father, then a Lieutenant in the USAFFE. He didn't know my father had smelled him coming, and hotfooted it to the mountains. On the second night, while catnapping, the Nip became aware of something slowly slithering across his shin. Realizing it was a python, he woke up with a start, shook it off his leg, and rushed pellmell down the branches, only to run smack into the Agtà. The latter calmly stubbed his cigar out on the sniper's cheek.

Apocryphal or not, the story lent our grove a certain cachet. The Japanese soldier was an outsider, fair game for our ghosts. Only bona fide Mango Boys could loll around in our tree house; we, and we alone, had as much right to the place as they did.

Other guys built better tree houses up in *their* mango trees. None of those ever acquired the fame and prestige of ours.

Since we were the Mango Boys and there could be no other, rival gangs had to content themselves with pretentious names like D'Young Pioneers or Los Indios Guapos.

Our greatest frustration was our lack of success in luring girls up to the tree house. We had girls hanging out and singing with us on the benches often enough, but none of them had the agility required to clamber up to the abode of the trueblue Mango Boys. So we regaled them with outlandish tales. We told them the Agtà had the power to turn us into bats if we slept in the tree house on the night of the harvest moon. Go to sleep lying supine on the boards, wake up hanging upside down from a twig at the treetop.

Or eat too much and go up the tree house to fall asleep on a full stomach, like an python engorged, and wake up with molting reticulate skin.

The tales got taller as the bonfires grew in that time of year when the mango trees required smoke offerings to induce flowering. Only the oldest men could tend the ritual fires so we kept to the biggest tree, on our benches or in the tree house. That tree was male and could not bear fruit, producing only token flowers. Into the bonfire built under it the old men would toss in leaf after cured leaf of storebought tobacco, for the Agtà. Once a couple of the guys surreptitiously added some wilted marijuana plants they had stolen from the storeroom of a law enforcement agency which had confiscated those from a plantation in a lightning raid. We thought it might cause the girls to bloom. For the rest of the day everyone went around in a lightheaded stupor, eyes glazed, pupils dilated. Those in the tree house dropped off to sleep. They later reported fantastic dreams.

The mangoes weren't for us to eat off the trees. The produce was bought wholesale, every year, by fruit dealers from out of town. Sales would be contracted when the trees flowered, and the buyers would come back in a month to cover each individual fruit with paper as protection from pests. With the crop needing five months to mature and ripen, they protected the trees from us with barbed wire around the trunks. We considered it an insult. We didn't care for green mangoes, that being a delicacy for pregnant women, but we'd eat them as an act of defiance. We'd slice a green mango into juliennes and dip them into *ginamos*, a thick salty condiment made from fermented small fish. The more progressive among us claimed green mangoes tasted better with *bago-ong*, the pungent Tagalog version of *ginamos*, because *bago-ong* smelled horrible, and cut the sourness of the mango better. They'd snicker while saying this, meaning there was another reason. The ones in the know never elucidated. It was something for the other guys to figure out or puzzle over. Some would just laugh coarsely, to make it look like they knew all about it.

The dealers returned to harvest the mangoes about a week before full ripeness, when the fruit was still green but committed to turning yellow. There were always a few that ripened ahead, and we were good at finding these and stealing them, no matter how inaccessible the branch they might be on. The best way to eat one was right there, where you found it, on the stem. And then leave the seed hanging. Like a bat had eaten through the paper.

With the fruit all sold off, the rains would come. The water seeped into the thirsty ground, to be sucked up by greedy roots. The sap then rose, in the mango trees oozing out of the bark in clear orange globules, like amber, turning dark after a day's exposure to air—very sticky to the touch. Vitality overflowed in us too, fire in the blood turning us touchy and impetuous—this being the time of year when unthinkable things were not only thought but actually done, when a guy might run away from home, or turn zealot and find religion, or blow a small fortune at the cockfights.

And when the rains had gone bad memories evaporated, leaving us to drift back to the tree house so we could bone up on romantic songs. Then off to serenade some girl, the young swain pressing his suit taking the lead vocals. Invariably a tonedeaf drinker, he would have to be cued in with the opening chord so he could get the pitch. We'd have two or three false starts if he was too drunk to get it right the first time. We would sing a Visayan ballad and the lead singer would invent a poetic *balak* to orate in the middle of the song while we hummed the melody. Then we'd do a song in English, which would reveal the thickness of his pronunciation. So we'd sing background harmonies as loud as we could, often drowning him out.

It was always worth it. Girls spurned our first advances as a matter of course, and had to be serenaded before a second try became feasible.

The girl would invite us in before rival suitors stoned us. After a few minutes we'd excuse ourselves one by one, leaving the girl alone with her beau. We'd resume the drinking at the tree house, refining the songs we didn't get to do. The lovestruck fool would catch up with us before the jug was empty.

Inevitably, there came a time when I couldn't join them for the post-serenade session. I had to study for an exam, and the next time it happened I had a thesis to write. After that there was always something or other, overtime on the job, late-night movies with the wife, 2 a.m. feedings. Then we migrated to a place where the nearest mango tree was a mile away and standing all by itself, not surrounded by a grove of female trees.

Seeing the old place only on occasional visits to my parents' house made the changes seem faster. The Mango Boys had grown up and become different things: a tricycle driver, a civil engineer, an airline employee, an illegal alien in California, a contract worker in Kuwait, a rebel priest in Mindanao. One of the girls we used to serenade had gone to Japan as a singer/entertainer in a bar called My Brother Leon and brought home a husband. He was of the *shinjinrui*, and they built a house on land they bought, cutting down a few of the mango trees to make room for a Zen garden.

One day, in an airconditioned bus to a distant city, I noticed a clump of mango trees ahead, a bowshot from the road. As it drew abeam, I saw a few guys on benches under it. A gust of wind blew its leaves aside, exposing a tree house with more guys and a guitar. They saw the bus at the same time and one of them, the guitarist, waved. *"Come hither,"* he sang, and I heard him right through the soundproof window. I couldn't make out their faces, but the way they were they looked just like us, and the guitarist was myself. It was as if the years had telescoped things and I was watching the scene through a time machine. The Mango Boys were all there. We had simply moved, having found which tree the Agtà and the python now haunted. My impulse was to climb up and join them for that last drink, but I was in a hurry and important appointments awaited me at my destination. Then a sudden squall, rain coming down in sheets, and as it fell behind, windlashed and wet, the tree all forlorn and wild-eyed.

# Kukri

Years had slipped by since last I went to the Bulawan Bazaar. Located in the old part of Cebu City and owned by a Bombay, as we called people from India, it had been doing business for as long as I could remember.

Now I barely recognized the proprietor. He had faded into old age. Had it been that long? I looked expectantly at him but I might as well have been invisible. It was disconcerting. In the old days he had always rushed forward to greet my father with a "Yes, sahib?" but now he turned his back and shuffled into an inner room.

He emerged a moment later, very much younger. He had been through a time machine. He was my age now, a man even younger than the proprietor as I remembered him from long ago.

"Yes, sahib?"

An illusion, of course; it was the old proprietor's son. He awaited my pleasure, seemed eager to haggle. I was keenly aware of some volatile power in him: the ability to transform himself from affable gentleman to consummate merchant at a moment's notice. I sensed I was at a disadvantage: my personality wasn't the kind that went for the jugular.

I had been saving up for a new watch, but now saw from the price tags that I couldn't afford the ones I liked. I pretended to be interested in the rare coins. I'd been into coin collecting in high school, when everyone had to have a hobby, and I still knew a thing or two about numismatics. In order not to leave without having bought anything, which might be bad form, I selected an old coin. It was a 20-centavo piece, sterling silver, in what I guessed to be Very Fine condition. I looked for its mintmark: D, S, or M. I found it had a tiny letter P.

I paid the Bombay what he asked for the coin. The transaction over, he effortlessly turned back into a good old boy. "So you have a coin collection," he bonhomied. I replied with pleasant noises, yes, I had a few gold coins, too, nothing very rare, no, I rarely had time to look at my coins now, I just bought the *veinte* on impulse. The coin was properly called the *peseta* but everyone in Cebu called it by the wrong Spanish word. I pronounced it *baynti* in the Visayan way, as the young Bombay had. He spoke the local language quite well, much better than his father did, with a *bugoy* accent, too.

"My name is Ganjabahadur Thapa."

"Juan Muraña," I said, giving the first monicker that popped into my mind, the name of a character in a story by some Latin American writer.

"Anything else I can do for you, sahib?"

"No, that will be all, thank you."

I turned to go.

"Oh, by the way," I said, turning back, "would you happen to have any knives for sale?"

"Knifes? No, I'm sorry, we don't sell knifes."

"Perhaps in the storeroom or somewhere?"

His sharp Indian eyes bored into mine.

"Sahib, down the street is the Sen Hiap Hing Department Store. I believe you can find some very good knifes there. Try the houseware section."

"Er, ah, that's not exactly the kind of knife I'm looking for."

"Then I am sorry to disappoint you, sahib. As you can see, we sell only watches and jewelry and assorted curios."

"Yes, of course. What I really mean is, it was the colonel who suggested you could help me."

"The colonel?"

"Col. Maning Segura. He did not actually tell me to come here, you understand. He just happened to mention your shop in passing."

"Col. Segura? Why didn't you say so at once? Now I understand. Well, sahib, perhaps you had better come inside."

He led the way into the back room, which turned out to be quite spacious. His father was nowhere to be seen. There had to be another exit, but I could not see where that other door might be.

The room looked like any sala, a rolltop desk with a bookshelf behind it, a rich carpet that covered half the parquet floor, modern furniture, curtains and Venetian blinds on the windows, on the walls a large Persian rug and two paintings (a Botong Francisco and an Ang Kiu Kok), antique Chinese jars and vases, a bronze Buddha, in a corner ledge a Santo Niño with an electric votive candle flickering before it, and pride of place given to two glass cabinets full of knives and bladed weapons.

It was warm in there. I could feel myself breaking out in sweat. I should have kept my damnfool mouth shut and left after buying the old coin. My host waved me to the sofa, switched on the electric fan, and adjusted its angle to favor me. The books on the coffeetable had all been lovingly jacketed in clear plastic: one on jeepneys, another on stone churches; one on the art of Amorsolo and another on Juvenal Sansó.

He began taking knives out of the cabinets to put on the table. I shoved the books aside to make more room. Careful not to show my ignorance, I didn't ooh or aah or ask the names of any of those knives. He had everything. It didn't seem farfetched to suppose he had the flint knife used by Joshua to circumcise the Israelites during their wanderings in the desert.

I picked up the survival knife, a twin of the one shown in *First Blood*, and tested its sharpness with my thumb.

"Just like Rambo's knife," I said.

"I saw that movie a dozen times," he said.

"Remember how in the movie the knife was so sharp sheets of bond paper could be dropped on it and they'd get sliced? It must have been a camera trick."

"It is no trick, sahib. But you must know how to sharpen the knife. It is not as easy as you might think. There is a correct way and a wrong way to sharpen a knife."

"Any bond paper around?"

"No, sahib, that is only for the movies. Paper is very bad for the steel blade. The paper molecules will wreck the alignments of the steel molecules on the cutting edge.

Then you have to resharpen the knife again. But I will show you a better test."

He tugged at a lock of his hair. Before my eyes, he dropped it across the sharp edge. Incredibly, the hair fell apart on opposite sides of the blade, having been sliced in two.

"The romantic way to test a blade," he said, "particularly a sword made in Toledo or Damascus, is with a silk scarf."

"Got a silk scarf? Or a silk handkerchief?"

"No, that is for sissies."

"Where did you get this *samurai*?"

"Excuse me, sahib, that is not a samurai, that is a *katana*. A samurai is a man, a Japanese warrior. No, no, don't draw it from the scabbard, you might cut off a finger without even knowing it. A samurai does not unsheathe his katana unless he is going to use it."

"So where did you get it?"

"They are souvenirs from the war. A Cebu guerrilla, one of Col. Segura's men in the Resistance, took it from a Japanese officer he had killed in combat. After the war, he sold it to my father, along with the *wakisazhi*."

"The what?"

"The wakisazhi, the shorter sword. You know, a samurai always wears two swords. Here is the other one."

"That's the one they use for *hara-kiri*, isn't it?"

"*Seppuku*."

"So both these swords are genuine."

It seemed he wasn't sure if I was stating a fact or being ironic. There had once been a fad for Japanese swords, and as a result imitation "samurais" had glutted the sidewalks of Cebu City for months.

"The Japanese take very good care of their katanas. They are handed down from father to son. They do not rust. They last for centuries. They are kept in a place of honor in the house, in a corner that is like a Shinto shrine."

"How much would you sell this for?"

"Those are not for sale. Some years ago a Japanese tourist came to Cebu to honor the exact place where his father had died, and to look for his father's swords. He placed classified ads in the local papers. He was the son of an Imperial Army captain killed in Cebu in 1943, and he was offering plenty of money for the swords. I am sure these are the very swords he was looking for. They fit the detailed descriptions in his ad."

"Why didn't you sell them?"

"Oh, we were strongly tempted. The *hapon*'s offer was about ten times what the swords might have fetched in an auction at Sotheby's.

"But Baba remembered how his business had been failing, then suddenly improved after he bought the swords. Most people know only about the katana and don't know about the wakisazhi. Not often can you get both swords. Baba said one sword by itself would not have much power, but the two swords together would retain some kind of magic, something of the samurai spirit.

"That *hapon*—I don't remember his name—actually found his way to the shop and asked many questions. The ex-guerrillas who had guided him to the place where his father was killed had heard that their old comrade had sold the swords to my father.

"Baba denied it. He knew the guy who sold him the swords had died a few years ago, of natural causes. Baba told the *hapon* we did not deal in swords, only in watches and jewelry."

"Didn't you feel obliged to return the swords to him? After all, he was only reclaiming his heritage. And why didn't you offer to sell for twice the price he quoted? He would probably have paid even that."

"Baba was not sure the tourist was really the Japanese officer's son. He told me later that the man did not have the aura of a true samurai. Better to keep the swords than to sell them to such a man."

As for his other knives, I noticed he had grouped the Muslim ones together. My knowledge of Muslim weaponry was limited to that decorative item so dear to the *nouveau riche*, the tacky miniature shield laden with bonsai swords. Now I had the real items before me.

"That is a *kris*," the Bombay told me. "That is a *barong*, this one is a *kampilan*, this a *talibong*. The big one over there is a *tabas*."

I saw that he also had the Batangas *balisong*, or fan knife, in several sizes. He had a set of throwing knives. He had a few bayonets, but no rifles. He had a Visayan *pinoti*. And there were many others I didn't recognize.

"Look at this kris, sahib. It is the kind with the wavy blade. The Muslims call this the *kalis seko*."

He showed me the jeweled hilt, the braid around the curved handle, and the fine steel of the sinuous blade.

"It has more jewels than a Swiss watch. This other kris, with a straight blade, is called the *kalis tul-id*."

I picked up a balisong and opened and closed it with one hand. It was well balanced, the moving parts falling into place very nicely. In street parlance the balisong was the "veinte-nueve" because the graceful way to flick it open was to make like you were writing the number 29 in the air. All tough guys knew how to open and close a balisong this way, with either hand. I'd learned the skill, along with certain vices, somewhere in the impressionable years of my misspent youth.

"The kampilan is what Lapulapu killed Magellan with. It is single-edged, and has a little fin at its end. To use the technical term, it has a truncated distal end.

"The barong is shaped like a leaf, and has a broad backside. It is what they call lanceolate.

"The tabas is the heaviest of them all. It broadens at the distal end. Its curved handle is long and heavy, because it has to counterweight the blade. The tabas is never ornamented. Its best use is for beheading people. It is the one the Muslims use for executions."

"What's this?"

"That is the *kukri*."

A single piece of metal. Unlike most knives, which consist of a metal blade and a wooden handle. The handle rounded and shaped to fit a man's grip. The blade as hooked as a Jewish nose at the backside. Curved on the inside, the cutting edge. I hefted it.

"Heavy. It must weigh a kilo."

"Slightly more than that, sahib. A kilo is 2.2 pounds, or about 2 pounds and 4 ounces. The kukri weighs exactly 2 pounds and 14 ounces."

"Feels like it's the handle that weighs 2 pounds, and the blade only 14 ounces."

"They thought at first that it was a farm implement."

"Who did?"

"The first British soldiers to see it. In 1814. In the Nepal War."

"The Nepal War? Oh, I see. This must be the knife those Nepalese Gurkhas use. I didn't know it looked like this. I always thought it had a straight blade. If I remember right, this thing slit quite a few Argentine throats in the Falklands War."

"You are right, sahib. It also slit German and Japanese throats in World War II. It slit Turkish throats in Gallipolli in 1915, Afghan throats in 1879, and even Indian throats in Calcutta in 1857."

"The Sepoy Mutiny? You mean the Gurkhas go back that far?"

"Even farther. The British Army has been recruiting them since 1816."

"How did they get to fight the Germans?"

"In Tunisia, 1943. With the 8th Army. Against the Afrika Korps."

"And the Japanese?"

"In Burma, 1943. With Orde Wingate and the Chindits."

"How come you know so much about them?"

"I am an admirer of the Gurkha. The are so valiant that in 1915 the British King made them eligible for the Victoria Cross. Since then they have won many Victoria Crosses. But most of all, they are my countrymen."

"You, a Gurkha? But you're an Indian. You're a Hindu. Vaishya caste, isn't it? Your family came from Calcutta."

A glazed look had come over his eyes.

"My family lived in Calcutta for two generations before coming to this country. It's true that we were Hindu by religion. But we are really from Nepal. We are Gurkha. And we belong to the highest caste, the kshatriya. Please do not call us vaishya. That is a lower caste."

"Are you putting me on? Nepalese people belong to the Mongol race, like the people of Mongolia or Tibet or Bhutan. You don't look like that at all. You look like an Iranian."

"The Gurkha were a Mongoloid tribe, as you say. But unlike the Tibetans, they were not Buddhist. They followed the Hindu religion. That's why Gurkha men always looked for wifes from the Rai or Limbu tribes. Same religion, Hindu. Different race. Aryan. Then the Muslim invasion of India drove Rajput refugees into the Gurkha lands. Gurkha men began taking brides from the Rajput. Better than marrying a Nepalese woman from the Chetri, Magar, or Gurung tribes, who may be Mongoloid but are Buddhist. Most Gurkha are Mongol, that is true, but today many of us look Aryan."

"I don't understand it. Isn't Hinduism just like Buddhism? Hindus revere the cow because Buddha once returned to the world and took the form of a cow. So what's the difference?"

"I don't understand it, either. My father converted to the Catholic faith. I was baptized when I was a baby."

"Is that so? I thought you were one of those Hare Krishnas. Well, well. A Catholic Gurkha. I suppose your secret dream is to enlist in the British Army?"

"No, I have to stay here and run the shop. My father will be retiring soon. But if they ever form an auxiliary Gurkha unit here, I might join. Of course that will not happen, because there are no other Gurkha in Cebu. But it would be nice to be a *havildar* in any of the Gurkha Rifles."

"Why don't you form your own unit, anyway? You could call it the Kukri Klux Klan."

"What?"

"Nothing. What's a *havildar*?"

"A sergeant. Gurkha units always use Indian ranks, like *naik* for corporal, *jemadar* for lieutenant, or *subedar* for captain."

"About this kukri, how did you get it? Has it been used in combat?"

"My father got it from his cousin, Bhudibal Rana, a subedar-major in the 13th Gurkha Rifles. This kukri has slit the throats of twelve men and beheaded two others."

"Too bad it's all metal. If it had a wooden handle, your father's cousin might have marked every kill with a notch."

"Unlike wooden handles, sahib, metal handles never come off. The weight of the handle adds to the momentum of your stroke, so it takes just a single stroke to behead your enemy. A flick of the wrist. After the Japanese tasted the kukri in Burma in 1943, they became terrified of it."

"That's funny. They weren't afraid of guns, but they were afraid of the pinotì of the Cebu guerrillas in World War II."

"Yes, Col. Segura told us about that. Even after Hirohito's broadcast, the *hapones* in Cebu would surrender only to the Americans who had just arrived. They wouldn't surrender to the Cebu guerrillas whose pinotì knives were all aching for revenge."

I stood up to go. "I'll buy that pinotì," I said. "How much is it?"

He named an outrageous amount. I realized it was meant to be unrealistic. I was now supposed to make an equally ridiculous counteroffer, and we could then begin haggling. It was an ancient art of which he had to be a master.

"What do you take me for, an utter ignoramus? I could buy a pinotì at the Carbon market for half that price."

"Why don't you buy one at Carbon, then?"

"I only came here because Col. Segura spoke so highly of your shop. Now I'm not so sure. I'm not even sure of the quality of your goods."

"I assure you, sahib, everything we sell is of the highest quality."

"What about this coin you sold me? Here, look. Look at its mintmark."

He took it and peered at it for a moment.

"Yes, I see it. The letter P. So, P is for Philadelphia. This coin was obviously minted in Philadelphia."

"Was it?"

"As you know, sahib, all American coins have mintmarks. There is the letter D for Denver, S for San Francisco, C for Carson City, M for Manila. The Carson City mint lasted only a few years before it closed down in the 1840s. The Manila Mint opened in 1936 but was destroyed in the war, in 1942. So in the typical collection most American coins are from Denver, San Francisco, or Philadelphia."

"The Philadelphia mint," I very slowly said, "does not use a mintmark. Coins struck in Philadelphia are not supposed to have mintmarks."

"Oh, really? But sometimes they do. One example is the 1943 Lincoln penny, which was made of steel rather than copper."

"All right, on rare occasions they did use the P mintmark. But not for the Philippine Commonwealth 20-centavo coin of 1938. This coin is a fake."

"No, no, you're wrong. That's a very rare coin, and I should have sold it to you for a very high price. Unless you are accusing me of peddling counterfeit goods?"

"I am. I do so accuse you. It's a goddamned fake."

He glared at me. He was turning purple. I could see pure hatred in his eye.

"You also lied about your caste. The kshatriya isn't the highest. The highest caste is the Brahman."

Suddenly his face broke out in a gleeful, mocking smile. He had taken hold of the kukri. I lunged forward and grabbed the nearest knife, the pinotì.

We circled each other warily.

The carpet underfoot seemed to be Afghan. I had no shield; my left arm would have to do.

He made a wicked slash, but my reflexes were good, and I leaped backwards to put my body out of range by a fraction of an inch.

I saw an opening and thrust at him. He parried with the kukri. The clash of metal upon metal rang loud, reverberating in my bones.

The Persian rug shifted, and the old Bombay stumbled in. The rug had been hung over a secret door.

My adversary dropped his knife, and then I let go of mine, too. They made muffled thuds on the Afghan carpet.

The old man snarled at his son in a strange language.

Ganjabahadur Thapa hung his head and said something in a sheepish tone.

"I am sorry," the proprietor told me. "I hope you were not hurt?"

"Oh, it's nothing."

"My son has a short temper. He is very hotheaded."

"But Baba, he said the Brahman is the highest caste."

The old man sighed.

"The kshatriya caste, the warrior caste, has always been the highest. In the Vedas it is the highest. But a thousand years ago, the Brahmans simply proclaimed that their caste was the highest. We have never accepted that."

"What was that you were speaking to him, Bengali?"

"No. Gurkhali."

"I was going to buy that pinotì, but now I've changed my mind. I'd like to buy that kukri instead."

"It's not for sale," said Ganjabahadur Thapa.

"Take it," his father said. "Take it with my compliments. I give it to you."

"But Baba—"

"&%r#zh@*gk$!"—a sharp look, and the son was silenced.

At the shop counter the proprietor slid the kukri into its scabbard and wrapped it up with brown paper and string. I offered to pay, hoping he wouldn't charge more than I had on me. He shook his gray head, dismissing my bid with a wave of his hand.

"Come back soon, Muraña," said Ganjabahadur Thapa, "when you've become very good with that kukri."

"I will," I promised. "Get some practice with that pinotì."

His eyes burned into me from behind. Not once did I look back.

# Glossolalia

*(after John Barth)*

## 1

Summer moon cresting the heel stone creeps into darkness, the eclipse foretold on the eve of his death, my father's, in battle. For nineteen years I kept the count, by sevens and thirteens, around the fifty-six holes. Outside this hallowed earthwork circle my woman wails, my children flee. What must I sacrifice to yon lost god, she who knows my secret and my sin?

## 2

Dinhi lang, daplin sa dagat, taliwalà sa duhá ka sapâ. Nahabilin na ngadto ang Maja Pahít, mga dilì ingon natò, mangdukò sa buhî ug sa gahum ni Shiva. Magpadayon pa usab dinhi ang tabunon nga Vijayâ. Mga datù, mga manggugubat! Bisag isugbô, atò g'yud ni!

## 3

Ay, buhay, talon na naman, nahulog na rin ang aking takot. Ang target disk ngayon mukhang Haydee Yorac; kung high score, beso kay Erap, Jos ko, ano ba yan? Mga babae ngayon ay puede na ngà sa PMA, at walang magkukudeta. Kung hindì bumukas ang parasyut, sasakalin kita, koronel!

# Stonehenge

*for Edilberto K. Tiempo*
*(1913-1996)*

It wasn't so much his jaded air as his diffidence. A typical Englishman, he affected boredom at most times and in trying times kept a stiff upper lip. Durrant, however, had perfected a cynical sort of *sang-froid* that thoroughly disgusted me.

"A nice drive in the *bracing* country air," he said, emphasizing the key word in a way that made me wince. "Salisbury always seemed to me such a *windy* plain. Perfect antidote to London, wouldn't you say?"

"Your name isn't English, is it? Sounds French to me." Most people hated non sequiturs, and I thought to keep him off balance thus.

"Quite right," he admitted. "Norman French. But after nearly a thousand years, it's *echt* English now. Is your name Mexican?"

I had to admire his adroitness, albeit grudgingly. He was pulling my leg in his quiet way. Like most Filipinos I had a Spanish name, but mine was also infamous in Mexico.

The Wessex countryside was ideal for night driving. There being some eighty miles to cover, and it being imperative that we reach our destination before sunrise, we had left London at midnight, giving up all thought of sleep. I should have been driving, as my International Driver's License was valid for the UK and I was in fine fettle, while Durrant had had a drink or two at his club and was none the better for it. But when pressed I had been forced to admit I'd never been down west before. However, I was fairly certain I could find the way.

Well, he had told me very gravely, driving on the *wrong* side of the road in the *wee* hours would (here he paused for effect) *discomfit* me. That had settled the matter.

As we were getting into the car I muttered something about being none the worse for drink. Durrant pretended not to have heard. Neither of us bothered with the seatbelts. He lit a cigarette. He switched on the ignition. He slammed the stick into second gear and floored the accelerator, laying rubber as the vehicle screeched off like the villains' getaway car in a Ronnie Ricketts movie. He drove too fast. He braked suddenly at intersections. I suspected the idea was to make me bump my head on the dashboard. I hardly listened when he broke the silence after ten miles and briefed me on the route.

Our general direction, so he gave me to understand, was west or southwest. There was a new highway, the M400, which led straight to Bristol, but it meant going through a tunnel from Bristol to Salisbury. Durrant would opt for the old road, the A344. One kept watch for the place where it forked: to the left would be the A303. The right way was to continue on the A344. The henge was west of Amesbury and north of Salisbury town; it dominated Salisbury Plain, some seven miles from the town with the famous Salisbury Cathedral...

Had it been entrusted to me, I would probably have confused the placenames or interchanged the road numbers. None of it mattered now. Durrant was driving.

The whole thing had started off as a lark. With my visa due to expire in a few days, I had wistfully remarked that I had seen Portobello Road, the Tower of London, Madame Tussaud's, and several pubs, but had yet to see any of Britain's henges.

"My dear boy," Durrant then said, "wouldn't be proper now, would it? Perfect time to see one, too, summer solstice almost upon us. Hopefully, the weather will cooperate for once. We've been having cloudy Midsummer Days the past few years, but this might be the lucky year."

"Things are piling up back home," I said. "Perhaps I should take an earlier flight. There's one tomorrow."

"Utterly unthinkable. Mustn't leave England without having seen its henges. Obligatory tourist spots, you know. Although I don't know that I would have missed much if I hadn't seen Magellan's Cross, the Lapulapu Monument, or the Taoist Temple. Now the girlie bars and honky-tonks, those I wouldn't have missed for all the world. Fantastic places. Nothing like those around here. Not even in Soho."

He was treading dangerous ground, alluding to his stay in Cebu. I had been careful—a matter of *delicadeza*—to steer clear of that subject.

The henge appeared without warning. One moment we were driving through ordinary farmland, the next moment there it was. Our headlights, as if by sleight of hand, suddenly conjured up the Heel Stone on the left side of the road. Beyond it, standing in a circle, a majestic array of silent stones, silhouetted against the night sky and the stars. It was much bigger than I had always imagined.

"This road goes on to Avebury," Durrant said, "where there's a bigger henge. Would you like to go there instead? Only a few miles now."

"No," I said, "Stonehenge will do."

I glanced at my watch: 1:30 AM, Daylight Saving Time. That meant 12:30 AM, Greenwich Mean Time. I had adjusted quickly enough to the time difference, but somewhere in my vitals it was already half past eight in the morning. Philippine time was eight hours ahead of GMT, and my circadian rhythm had not quite reconciled itself to the change. My stomach had never left Cebu. Now it was grumbling for breakfast.

Durrant parked the car some distance away. "Used to be understood," he said, "that cars should be parked where they couldn't be seen from the henge. They'd spoil the view otherwise. But now too many tourists, the Yanks specially, seem unaware of that convention."

The sky was ablaze with stars; a mild breeze blew from the north.

"Thank heaven for that wind," Durrant said. "There won't be any fog, then. That wind will blow it off."

He opened the boot and took out a case of British beer. There was no icebox. I remembered that the English were inordinately fond of warm beer.

"I know you like your San Miguel beer ice-cold," he said, "but I think you'll find this porter quite good as it is. Must be fifty degrees right now, give or take a few. Even with no allowance for the wind-chill factor."

Obviously he was as accurate as a thermometer. He was also a show-off, daring me to disprove his estimate of the temperature. I worked it out in my head: something like 10° Celsius. Too cold for me but just right for the porter beer, which I found to be full-bodied and creamy. A beer lover's delight. Somehow it seemed colder than the air. I pulled my jacket tighter around me.

"We're actually rather early," he said. "The summer solstice isn't till tomorrow. The alignments won't be at their best."

"It should be good enough," I said. "But we left London on June 20, just before midnight. Today is June 21. Doesn't the solstice fall on June 21? Today?"

"Almanac says June 22."

"Perhaps it's better that way. I've heard this place gets crowded at sunrise on Midsummer Day. Now there won't be anyone else standing by the Altar Stone at first light."

I turned out to be wrong about that. As we were getting to the last of the beer a bus drew up and disgorged a group of elderly couples led by a young man. They headed for the ruins.

"Good morning," we greeted those who passed closest to us.

"Gut mourning," they replied.

"German accent," Durrant said. "Tourists."

"From which part of Germany?" I asked.

"Could be from Austria. Or Switzerland."

"You mean you can't tell the difference between Schweizerdeutsche and Osterreichischedeutsche?"

"Drink up," he said. "It's a quarter of four. Sky's fading."

I glanced up. Indeed, almost imperceptibly, the velvet black of the sky was fading into blue.

"What time is sunrise?"

"Four-thirty."

"I mean, according to the almanac?"

"Four twenty-seven and thirty-two seconds."

Daylight Saving Time, of course, if tongue-in-cheek. By local sun time, 3:30 AM. That seemed too early, but this part of England lay at about 50°N. The extreme latitude allowed an extremely premature sunrise. In Cebu, at 10°N, sunrise never came earlier than 5:30.

We followed the tour group to Stonehenge. The guide led them down the road until they reached the Heel Stone, where they turned into the Avenue. We crossed the Causeway behind them, filed past the Slaughter Stone, and entered the Sarsen Circle. The tourists walked around the trilithons. Durrant and I went into the Sarsen Horseshoe and stood by the Altar Stone.

The tour guide meandered around the Bluestone Circle, zigzagging inside and outside of it, his wards meekly following him. He kept up a running commentary, probably an oft-rehearsed lecture.

"Stonehenge consists of two concentric circles of upright stones surrounding two concentric ellipses, the whole surrounded by a double earth wall and ditch, about 370 yards in circumference. It has an entrance at the northeast which proceeds in the form of an avenue, guarded on each side by a wall and a ditch, for a distance of 594 yards, after which it divides, one branch going eastward up a

hill, between two groups of barrows, and the other leading northwest to the cursus 300 yards distant. That cursus,
or racecourse, is a stretch of flat land one and three-quarter miles long, and 110 yards wide."

"He sounds just like the bloody encyclopædia," Durrant
said.

"He must love this dolmen," I said.

"I beg your pardon, this is a henge, not a dolmen. A
dolmen is a tomb. Stonehenge was never used as a burial
place."

"Oh, a cromlech, then."

"We prefer to call it a henge," he sniffed.

"Two kinds of stone," the guide was saying, "were used
to construct Stonehenge. The massive menhirs are sarsen
stones, each weighing 35 or 40 tonnes, with the biggest
ones being as heavy as 50 tonnes. Sarsen is a kind of sand-
stone that's harder than granite. The effort it took to dress
these stones cannot have been short of phenomenal."

With no effort at all I dressed the sarsens in my mind:
I saw them clad in homespun gingham or calico dresses—
tartans, plaids, polka dots, and checks.

"Imagine the effort," the guide went on, "it took to
haul the dressed sarsens 24 miles from the Marlborough
Downs."

He patted a nearby bluestone.

"The smaller stones are bluestones, dolerites and rhyo-
lites from the Prescelly Mountains in Wales. Each one
weighs a tonne and a half. They were transported from
Pembrokeshire, 250 miles away. The most likely route
would have been by way of Milford Haven to Bristol, up

the Avon to Bath, then overland to Salisbury Plain. Rugged terrain, full of small streams and bogs..."

"He's never heard of Merlin the Magician," Durrant said. "All it took was Merlin's magic. He made these stones *fly* through the air. All the way here from Wales."

"Three different races of men," the guide was droning on, "centuries apart, built Stonehenge. Thus we speak of Stonehenge I, II, and III. It's really three different structures. The later races each built upon and added to the existing structure..."

None of it was new to me. The lecture sounded like bits and pieces of things I seemed to have read before. What books? Which authors? I couldn't remember. Lockyer, I supposed. Hawkins, too, or was it Hoyle?

Durrant of course probably knew much more about Stonehenge, as he did about most things. He was that type. He had the air of someone to whom these stones would speak, if he but gave them leave. However, he wasn't one to parade his knowledge. I would have to goad him into argument. The crudest way was to fall into little errors, allowing him the opportunity to correct me.

"I can't imagine how the Druids managed to raise those heavy stones atop the lintels," I said. Even my terminology was wrong.

He blinked.

"Very likely," he said shortly, "they piled up a lot of scaffolding under a lintel, raising it one level at a time, until they got it atop the pillars." He lifted his eyebrows a fraction of an inch, dismissing the other part of my statement. "But not the Druids. Stone Age men built this a couple of millennia before the Druids arrived in Britain. Everyone knows that, of course."

"Of course," I said, unsure if he could detect the small note of triumph that had crept into my voice. Eager to press home the advantage, I now decided to take the orthodox position. Perhaps it would exasperate him.

"Obviously," I said, "the races which came later were more advanced, and improved on the crude structure they found."

*"Au contraire,"* he said. "In all likelihood the first builders were the most advanced, possessing the knowledge to build a henge capable of predicting both lunar and solar eclipses. The later builders, by comparison, had little more than brute force going for them. Oh, they could dress and transport huge blocks of stone. They could fit 30-ton lintels atop 23-foot pillars with mortise-and-tenon joints. They could join lintel to lintel with tongue-and-groove joints. And they knew how to employ the principle of entasis. But they were not necessarily the equal of their predecessors as astronomers."

"My dear Durrant, that is a revelation indeed. You must enlighten me."

"Stonehenge I," the guide was saying, "was built circa 2800 BC, when the Beaker People lived in this area. It consisted of the ditch twelve feet wide, six feet deep, and 320 feet in diameter, the earthen ring, the Aubrey holes, and seven stones. It is perhaps not proper to call it Stonehenge at all as it had hardly any stone to speak of. What they built was merely a henge, a circular temple..."

"His lecture doesn't include the post holes," Durrant told me, "nor the wooden pegs stuck into the Aubrey holes."

"Mortise-and-tenon joints," I repeated. "Tongue-and-groove joints. Tang and clevis. Damned if I know the difference."

"You have heard of entasis, haven't you?"

"It's a sort of optical illusion? And the Greeks applied it when they built the Parthenon?"

"You've got the idea. The Greeks knew that straight lines in large buildings create optical illusions. Vertical lines bend, horizontal lines sag. To compensate for this, they made sure the columns of the Parthenon are not straight. Had they been, the Parthenon would have looked topheavy. Those columns swell slightly in the middle, and taper off towards the top. So too with the standing sarsens here. They swell in the middle and taper off towards the top. Entasis practiced centuries before the Greeks discovered the principle. A degree of sophistication unknown in any other henge in Europe."

"I suppose you're going to tell me why they stuck posts in the Aubrey holes?"

"One of this henge's great mysteries. The 56 Aubrey holes certainly have to do with the moon. Not the phases of the moon; those are too obvious. What isn't so obvious is that lunar eclipses fall into 19-year patterns. To be more precise, the cycle is about 18 years and two-thirds. Three such cycles equal 56.

"You stick a post in an Aubrey hole where it aligns with the rising full moon as seen from the Altar Stone. Next full moon, stick another post...the moon will have moved, and you'll have to use another hole. Rather like a giant version of that children's game of yours, *sungka*. If you do it long enough, you may discover a pattern. Then you might find yourself able to predict which hole should be used next. In the end you'll find that certain holes get to be used only when there's going to be an eclipse."

"And if you do it with the sun, you can predict solar eclipses, too?"

"Exactly. But here's what isn't so well known. Solar eclipses can only be viewed inside the narrow track described by the moon's shadow."

"Oh, everybody knows that. That's why scientists fly off to distant corners of the globe to catch solar eclipses. Then it turns out to be a cloudy day, and they never see anything of it at all."

"Right. Well, the alignments here at Stonehenge allow you to predict even the solar eclipses that are not visible in England."

The young man from the Tourist Bureau was now on the subject of the original seven stones at Stonehenge I.

"The Heel Stone," he was enumerating, "the two Gateway Stones, and the four Station Stones."

He pointed to four spots in the distance. The Station Stones, what remained of them, were at different points near the outer circle of the Aubrey holes, forming a wide rectangle.

"The four Station Stones mark the rectangle described by the moon's cycles. The sacred moonswing, it's called.

"One of the Gateway Stones has been lost. The other has fallen, and is popularly known as the Slaughter Stone. Mistakenly, I believe, for there is no evidence of human sacrifice here.

A professorial-looking German tourist interrupted him.

"But did not the Druids practice human sacrifice here, *ja?*

The guide didn't bat an eyelash.

"Yes, but in oak groves. Not in Stonehenge, which wasn't their temple to begin with."

It was much lighter now, and fingers of light pointed to the spot where the sun would rise.

"Speak of the Devil," said Durrant, glancing down the road.

They were coming in a merry procession, a whole coven of them. All in long white robes, led by a piper, to whose eerie music they were dancing. I looked closer: not a flute, but a recorder. Made of bone. A Stone Age fife.

"They come every year," Durrant told me. "For the Midsummer sunrise."

"Are they for real?"

"No, I would think not. They certainly don't belong to the same order described by Julius Cæsar, if that's what you mean."

"Do they go through the same initiation rites?"

"The original 18-day ordeal? I hardly think any of them would survive it. I'm quite sure they're merely revivalists. Been having plenty of that since the 18th century. Since Dr. William Stukeley made antiquarianism fashionable."

The "Druids" were inside now, in the eight-foot-wide walk between the Sarsen and the Bluestone Circles, dancing as they went clockwise around the henge. The circumference of that walk was about 300 feet.

"Did the Druids, I mean the real ones, accept women into their order?"

"Why do you ask? Oh, never mind, don't tell me. It's because of that girl with them."

He had seen her, too.

"But to answer your question, no, not by a bloody sight they didn't. They were dyed-in-the-wool male chauvinist pigs."

"You're mixing your metaphors."

"Am I? Well, metaphors were made to be mixed, I always say. Just as promises were made to be broken."

"You mean hymens were made to be broken."

"If you say so."

"That girl's a fine example of a classic Celtic beauty. Is black hair as common among the Celts as red?"

"Quite. It becomes her, too."

Neither of us had said what was obvious, that the Celtic girl who came with the "Druids" was a dead ringer for Diane, the girl who had come between us in Cebu. I suddenly found myself transported back to Cebu, to Fuente Osmeña, and so, I felt sure, had Durrant. Stonehenge, or maybe the Sarsen Circle, was about the same diameter, and the circular skating rink at Fuente Osmeña would fit nicely into the Bluestone Circle. It was early evening, we were going 'round and 'round on rented roller skates, Diane and I...and that was where she first met Durrant, too. While skating.

Durrant and I had known each other, casually, for a few weeks. He was a consultant for an engineering firm, and worked on the construction of a building. The company I worked for would be renting office space in that building, and I was there to oversee things on behalf of my employers, who had very specific ideas about the little details: the sprinkler system, the air conditioning, the plumbing, the restroom fixtures, the wall paneling, the telephone and computer lines...

I got to Fuente Osmeña fifteen minutes late, and saw that Diane was not alone. She was skating with a foreigner...why, it was that British guy I had seen around the construction site.

"Oh, you two know each other?" Diane asked. Then, aside to me, "I don't know who he is, he just started skating beside me, doing little stunts around me. He's a show-off, really."

"Diane, I'd like you to meet Paul," I said. "Paul Durrant. Consultant for Atlas-Itochu. I see him around the new building. Paul, Diane."

*"Enchanté."*

I thought he was going to kiss her hand next, but he wasn't that Old World. "I say, how does beer and pizza sound to everyone? All this skating has made me quite thirsty."

We made a cordial threesome, but he had a car and I didn't, so he got to take her home. He offered to drop me off, too, but I mumbled something about having to go downtown to... .

Neither of them even waited to find out exactly where I had to go. They weren't that interested. Perhaps they only had eyes for each other, or perhaps everyone in the big city always cultivated an air of nonchalance. None of their business where I was off to, and none of mine where they were off to...going home, of course. He was drop-ping her off at her place. It was along the way. That was all there was to it.

I brooded about it for the next few days. I had not stopped brooding about it. I was brooding about it still.

Most of my waking hours since that day had been spent in a daze. My manager's voice seemed very far away when he informed me that the company was sending me to London to attend a conference. Shuttling to Manila to get the visa, preparing the position paper, packing my bag—abstract exercises, all. Durrant was attending, too, and I was keenly aware of the fact that he would be leaving Cebu two days after me. Those two days weighed heavily on my mind. They were a noose around my neck, attached to a millstone I held in my hands, and my legs were willing me to go and jump off.

I had held off asking Durrant about it. I had formulated the exact phrasing of such a delicate question many times in my head: very casual, just another bit of pointless small talk, as random as a comment on the weather.

"What did you do, those last two days in Cebu?"

To my dismay, I realized I had spoken aloud.

He looked as if he hadn't heard. A Visayan would have turned to me and asked "Ha?" to require confirmation of something he had heard very well. Sometimes it exasperated me, but at least it allowed one to rephrase. Or one could change one's mind and say, "Oh, nothing."

"The usual things," Durrant said. "Nothing much."

The sun broke through the clouds on the horizon and sent a beam of golden light straight to the upraised arms of the Druid high priest at the Altar Stone. The Druids had gathered around the Altar Stone, grouping naturally into a semicircle as they aligned themselves with the Bluestone Horseshoe. Two of them were leading Diane's lookalike from the Heel Stone down the Avenue to the Altar Stone.

"An old ritual, new players, a *coup de foudre*. Rollicking good time."

"Who, you?"

"No, ah, those Druids over there."

His awkward denial only served to confirm it. In the English language there was no difference between the singular *you* and the plural *you*, but he had chosen to shift the burden of the pronoun to the Druids, a plural quantity. He had not been agile enough to find a singular quantity. I was sure he had understood my "you" to be plural. I was sure the rollicking good time was a slip of the tongue.

"What's a *coup de foudre*?"

"Oh, that's French for a clap of lightning."

I waited for him to say more.

"Let's move on, shall we?"

The Druids were "sacrificing" Diane at the Altar Stone. They had lain her out on the sarsen slab. She kept deathly still, slack and supine, eyes closed. The high priest brandished a knife, holding it with both hands high over his head, ready to plunge it into her heart. The German tourists were agape with wonder. The scene must have awakened some atavistic fervor in their own hearts, summoned racial memories of having sacrificed to their own gods in just this way. In many ways, I thought, the Norse gods and the Celtic gods were not so different from each other.

But I was deluding myself, keeping my mind on scholarly matters when I knew very well it seethed with thoughts closer to hand. My French was slightly better than Durrant might have supposed. I knew *coup de foudre* literally meant a "clap of lightning," but I also happened to know it was the French idiom for "love at first sight."

I clenched and unclenched my hands as I followed Durrant back to the car.

"It's all for show," he said. "There are policemen watching discreetly from the sidelines. Those Druids won't do anything foolish."

Useless small talk. Perhaps it was what kept the English so civilized, their talent for filling in awkward spaces with equally vacuous chatter. No other people made such a great production of talking about the weather.

"Could be rain in a few minutes," Durrant said. "Mornings this time of year are apt to produce sudden drizzles."

We got into the car, neither of us bothering with the seatbelts. He started the engine, kept it idling as he paused to light a cigarette, then leaned over to light mine.

"Thanks," I said out of habit, forgetting my resolve to maintain a sullen silence.

He was in no hurry. He drove slowly, more concerned with enjoying his cigarette than gaining speed. The Druids were frozen in tableau at the Altar Stone, the Germans still watching them in openmouthed awe. The high priest's knife remained poised over the vestal virgin's heart. As we passed by the northeast entrance, still in second gear, the first few drops of rain began spattering on the roof. Then they were streaking the windshield.

I rolled up my window as I craned my neck to watch people running from the Sarsen Circle, scattering about, seeking the shelter of their vehicles. They were all soaking wet.

"Poor devils," Durrant said as he shifted into third, then fourth, and then, scornful of the dangers of a slick road, fifth. "Wet, cold, and sopping miserable. Never knew what hit them."

# James, the Brother of Jesus

Santiago Ponce de Vedra was **44** that year, the year I moved into their village, which is to say some six years after his eldest brother Jesse was salvaged, and a couple of years after his elder brother Jude left for the Middle East. Jude had gone to Iran, but when last heard of had made his way to India.

Jesse, Jude, James: fine names for brothers, except that there was no James. Santiago didn't care for the Anglicized form of his name. He wasn't keen on translation. Nobody ever called him Tiago, either. He was Santiago and always had been. It wasn't that he was a tough guy; rather, he had a natural dignity that made it impossible for silly nicknames to stick to him.

To be sure, it wasn't the name his parents had wanted to give him. His father had favored the name Jacob, while his mother had insisted on James. At the baptism the priest had suggested a compromise: Santiago, a name that would go well with their surname, Ponce de Vedra.

Santiago was the third child, but only the second pregnancy: preceding him were the twins, Jesse and Jude. After him came the others: Reba, José Jr, Simon, and Mariel.

A large brood, typical of families in that village. Typical too was their mix of Anglo and Hispanic names.

At the time I moved into their village only Mariel, the youngest daughter and as yet unmarried, still lived in the old house with their widowed mother María. Jesse was dead. Jude was abroad. Reba, Joe Jr., and Simon had all married but were living nearby; on Saturdays they gathered for lunch in María's house, with their spouses and children.

His father, an architect who liked to describe himself as a carpenter, had died when Santiago was 12. José Ponce de Vedra could do anything a carpenter could, and Santiago remembered him as the sort of architect who helped out whenever things got hectic: sawing wood, hammering nails, doing the plumbing or stringing up the electrical wiring.

Santiago's mother nicknamed him James, just as she called Jude "Tommy," but they outgrew those baby names in their teens.

Jesse had been a rabble-rouser. He knew how to work a crowd. A master of mob psychology, he could whip the masses into a frenzy. He combined the talents of the Bible-Belt preacher and the political activist. Jesse was a zealot.

Santiago was none of these. He preferred the way of compromise. He too was a leader of men, but not in the obvious ways. After Jesse's death the mantle of leadership fell, practically by default, on Santiago's shoulders. Some factions however thought Jesse's widow should have succeeded to the role. It would have made for a classic situation, of course: the widow taking up her fallen husband's fight. It was an old tradition, old even by the time of Di-

ego and Gabriela Silang. I was old enough to remember
Magnolia Antonino running for the Senate in the 60s after
her husband, a Senator seeking reelection, was killed in a
helicopter accident. In the 80s a variation of that theme
propelled Cory Aquino to the Presidency in the aftermath
of Ninoy's assassination. But for Magda, the situation
wasn't quite so pat. These were the 70s, the martial law
years, and Jesse hadn't been in government, he had been
in the opposition. Jesse's erstwhile righthand man, Pedro
"Jun" Simon, led another faction. Jun's main drawback
was that he lacked Jesse's subtlety; Jun was a big man
physically but somewhat crude, and hot-tempered to boot.
And there was Pablo Tarsona, a johnny-come-lately whose
eloquence came close to Jesse's but whose ideals did not.

Santiago came to the leadership rather reluctantly. His
priority was preserving the ideals Jesse had died for, and
it seemed he would have to step in if only to keep the fires
burning.

Magda did not stay in the picture for long. A few months
after Jesse's death her uncle, José Armànde, took her to
distant France. Armànde's grandfather had been French;
he was heir to a vast tract of land in Provence. Armànde
was going to retire there. Some people said Magda had
been pregnant with Jesse's posthumous child. Supposedly
Reba had received a letter from Magda with the news that
she had given birth to a boy, whom she had named Jesse
after his father. Others, however, contended that it was
unlikely Magda would have written to Reba. Perhaps it
had been Armànde writing to his friend, old man
Nicodemo. Whatever the truth of the matter, the village
seemed to accept that Jesse's line lived on, albeit lost to us
in far-off Europe, where he would inherit Armànde's es-
tate. Perhaps he would return some day, when he was of

age, and prove he was his father's son, but the possibility seemed too remote, too far in the future, to think about.

In any divided party there are apostates and heretics aplenty, and a few who have kept the faith—or at least those were the terms they used, the names they called each other. At times the meanings were obscured, and I could not be sure who was which, but I think now that Santiago may have had a harder time keeping the faith than did Pablo espousing a heresy. I use the terms in a relative way: if Santiago kept closest to Jesse's ideals, then Pablo was the heretic who strayed into the temptations of other paths. But then change was sorely needed; Pablo was the first to adapt to new conditions, and the innovations he fostered probably ensured the party's survival. One tries not to be too harsh with Santiago, yet it must be admitted he was not at all the visionary his brother had always been.

Pablo attracted quite a following. Many defected from Santiago's camp and accepted Pablo's ideology. Pablo courted the wealthy and the powerful. Even Pedro Simon allied himself eventually with Pablo.

Santiago sometimes expressed the wish that Magda had stayed. His sister-in-law had a charisma of her own, and together they might have made a formidable team. But Magda and Jun Simon were not on good terms and Santiago, try as he might, could never reconcile the two. They differed on many issues, each so trivial as to be negligible, but when taken together amounting to quite a lot.

Pablo's arrival seemed opportune for Pedro Simon. A simple man, he was not very good at speechmaking or at handling crowds. Pablo became his spokesman, and the two of them made a pair. Pablo's arrival on the scene made it clear the balance of forces had changed. This galvanized Magda's decision to go into self-exile with her uncle.

Still, a sort of equilibrium was maintained, for a while at least. If Santiago could not attract enough adherents to form a critical mass, neither could Pedro Simon, even with Pablo at his side, acquire the stamp of legitimacy he so badly needed. He claimed that Jesse had left the reins to him. By way of bearing this out, he would quote verbatim long monologues Jesse had purportedly delivered to him. They sounded authentic: many of us were familiar with Jesse's rhetoric, and these speeches, couched in Jesse's peculiar phrasings, always harped on Jesse's favorite themes. But Jun Simon did not bring forth witnesses to testify that these indeed were Jesse's words, and he had nothing on paper, or even on tape. The absence of documentary proof was telling. Santiago at least had been endorsed by Jesse in the next-to-last plenary meeting the latter had attended, no matter that the younger brother had been reluctant to accept it. No one then could have foreseen Jesse's sudden death, although Jesse himself had often acknowledged the dangers his life was subject to.

The crisis did not come until I had lived in their village for a good eighteen years. Santiago was now 62 but otherwise had not changed much, except perhaps that his beard seemed to have grown grayer. Snap elections were called that year. Everyone knew it would be a farce, and indeed it was, but the "loser" refused to accept the results. This was not surprising; a losing challenger always accused the incumbent of cheating. This time however, a coup d'état took place. The incumbent was hounded out, and the rightful winner installed.

All this took place in the capital, far away from our little village in the hinterlands, but soon the repercussions reached us. Pablo was arrested, but to everyone's surprise he produced a foreign passport, a diplomatic one at that, and when the regional commander verified it with the consulate concerned, they confirmed that Pablo was indeed one of their foreign service officers. The military had no choice but to let him go.

Santiago, it seemed, would come into his own now. The new government had no time to hold local elections, which had been overdue, and chose the expedient of appointing officials to replace the elected ones whose terms were expiring. Santiago was appointed OIC of our village.

The mayor he was replacing refused to vacate the office. Santiago had his appointment papers, duly signed by all the proper authorities, but the old curmudgeon barricaded himself inside the office, said a mere piece of paper meant nothing to him, and that only a direct spoken order from the President would make him budge. He did not stop there. He was an accomplished demagogue. His skill in pandering to unruly crowds had helped him stay in office through the vicissitudes of different governments, and now he began making wild accusations against Santiago.

Santiago, he said, had infiltrated the foreigner Pablo into Pedro Simon's camp to spy on the latter. Santiago was in cahoots with the Reds and the rebel guerrillas.

It was all fabrication, but many of the people were easily swayed. Santiago, the old warhorse went on, was a heretic. He claimed to have been named after James, the brother of Jesus, and believed Jesus really had a brother, although our parish priest had said the Greek word for "brother" as used in the Gospels was often applied to cousins or close friends. Santiago interpreted passages like Matthew 13:53-57 and Mark 6:1-4 to mean that Jesus had four brothers and two sisters. Santiago preached that Jesus had a twin, and that this twin was the second figure from the left in Leonardo da Vinci's painting "The Last Supper."

This was a tissue of lies, for although Santiago went to church regularly, he kept his religion private and had never talked about the things the mayor was attributing to him. I doubted if Santiago could cite chapter and verse as the mayor had. But there was no stopping the codger. His voice had gone strident, and he had the whole mob hypnotized now.

Such blasphemies, he ranted, would in Biblical times have merited death. Death by stoning.

"Stone him!" yelled a fierce voice in the crowd, obviously a planted *agent provocateur*.

"Stone him!" echoed several other men, in voices as frenzied as those of Romans at the Colloseum.

I did not see who cast the first stone. I ran for a telephone, knowing the local police would be no help, and that I must call the regional command.

The mob, having stoned the life out of Santiago, had dispersed by the time the first troops arrived.

# Cadibarrawirracanna

His feathers were falling out a few at a time, and it irritated him. From his perch on the cliff edge he could hear the surf pounding on the rocks very far below. Usually a comforting sound, today it grated on his ears. He did not feel like flying. For a seabird, that was very odd.

He began the tedious task of preening, something that had to be done regularly: feathers were always fraying, and their barbs sprung apart all the time. He would run his beak along the edges of separated barbs and mesh them together again. Each barb was edged with many barbules, each barbule had numerous little barbicels, and each barbicel hooked onto its partner, exactly like a zipper.

Now and then, feeling an itch, he would tug at a feather. It often came off and then, curiously, the itchiness would transfer to its opposite number in the other wing. So he would tug at that until it, too, fell off. His tail feathers dropped off the same way, in symmetrical pairs. There were gaps in his wings and tail where the feathers had fallen out. New ones would soon grow in their place, but for the time being all his flying had to be done with reduced lift.

Molting was such a tiresome process. The ducks and the geese, always the practical ones, had stripped it down to simplicity itself: shed all the flight feathers, get it over and done with, grow them back as fast as you can. It was all right for them, they fed on fairy shrimp and tadpoles and water bugs and the roots of weeds in the muddy bottoms of ponds. They could afford to be flightless for a couple of weeks. Not him. He couldn't live on oddments or animalcules or such. He ate fish that he caught in the open sea. For that he had to keep flying. That was why his quill feathers always came off in matched pairs. It wouldn't do to become unstabilized. Still, flying with a few missing feathers always annoyed him. He couldn't get airborne from a standing start; he needed to run into the wind, or fall off a cliff. If the wind ever died down, takeoff with gaps in his wings would be chancy.

It never came to that. The wind was always fresh in the Bass Strait. Somehow, this only irked him further.

When starting out he always flew into the wind, so that on the return leg he would not have to fight it all the way home. But facing the wind at the outset seemed to use up most of his energy. Launching himself into the air took quite an effort, and that was only the beginning. Little by little it was getting harder to find fish, and every day he had to fly out farther than the day before.

There was a nip in the air, too. Temperatures had been gradually dropping over the past week, and he knew it would not be long now. Soon it would be time for the long flight. The moment his feathers had all grown back, he would be ready.

For now he was glad he had the wingspan to glide for hours on end without ever flapping his wings. He stretched nearly nine feet from wingtip to wingtip and only his cousins the albatrosses, some of whom boasted spans of eleven feet, had longer wings. Like them, he could stay aloft all day. He used the same method they did, the method his parents had taught him.

The winds over the sea were separated into two layers, with the dividing line at about the 50-foot level. Above that invisible line was the slow wind. Below it, right down to the wavetops, lay the fast wind.

There was a way to take advantage of this circumstance. One flew in circular patterns, dipping in and out of the two layers. The slow wind could sustain one's altitude if one headed into it—but not if he flew with it. It was in the downwind glide, never flapping one's wings, that the aerialist came into his own. As he slowly lost altitude he would wheel around. The trick was in the timing. When he had turned 180 degrees he would be down in the low layer, facing the fast wind. This gave enough lift to force him up into the high layer again, where he would wheel another 180 degrees and be gliding with the wind once more. Then he would repeat the cycle.

It was easy once he had got the hang of it, and when he could glide and soar in circles and figure 8s without ever getting tired, he knew he was in his element. He could stay in the air indefinitely—forever if he wished. The secret was his to keep.

The days wore on. Winter was coming to the southern hemisphere, and soon it would be time to migrate to other climes. On the other side of the world, in the northern hemisphere, summer was approaching. He and his fellows would rendezvous with it from thousands of miles away.

There was no definite day for the start of the long flight, but they would all know when it was time. An impulse would grab them, when their molting was done and the chicks hatched in the last breeding season grown strong enough to last the distance, and then they would simply go.

One day he woke up to find the impulse nudging him, saw it was taking hold of all of them, then with a squawk and a cheer that echoed everyone else's squawk and cheer, he had taken to the air. They were on their way.

He could not be sure exactly what that impulse was. Something in the air, or a certain shift of wind, or a sign from the sun or the stars, or perhaps some inner pull, triggered by hormones; whatever it was, like a gunshot it startled them into flight, and sent them winging northward.

He was used to flying alone, but for a voyage as arduous as this it felt good to be part of a flock. His father, who had flown the route many times and could be counted on to know the way, was the squadron leader. They flew in a tight group, like the geese, with the leader breaking the air out in front. The lead flyer's slipstream extended back at two angles, one to the left and the other to the right; the followers fell naturally into the places where the airflow made the flying easier, resulting in their V formation.

Flying at the forefront was exhausting work. When the lead flyer tired out he would drop back slightly, signalling a wingman to move up and take his place. Three or four of the adult males took turns as lead flyer, relieving each other every hour or so. The alternate leaders merely maintained course, speed, and altitude; it was the squadron leader's prerogative to initiate changes in any of these. They were flying north across Australia, and in the thin air at 15,000 feet they had worked up to almost 50 miles per hour, a good cruising speed they could keep up all day. They could go faster, but only at the risk of burning out.

They navigated by the sun, not so much by the actual sight of it as by the polarization of its light, so it did not matter if the sky was clear or overcast. They compensated continually, but without conscious effort, for the sun's gradual shift from east to west. It was all instinct. They could feel the earth's magnetic field, and could combine their sense of where North lay with the way the sun's light was polarized. At night, in addition to their feel for North, they could rely on the squadron leader's specialized knowledge of the stars. He himself had learned the names of a few stars, but he couldn't pinpoint them in the sky the way his father could: Canopus, Fomalhaut, Sirius; Lyra, Altair, Deneb.

His father had also learned, over the years, the important features and landmarks of the route. This was knowledge passed down the generations, with the difference that, unlike the things they knew by instinct, it was constantly being revised. Forests his ancestors had known for ages had somehow disappeared. Wetlands had dried up. Strange things had sprouted where land had been cleared or drained, ungainly structures inhabited by creatures who sometimes turned on birds and killed them. He was familiar with the curved stick some of those humans threw at birds. He knew the arrows they also employed, usually with a feather at the haft for irony, intended or not. And some of them had sticks that made sudden loud noises and killed before you knew what had hit you.

His flock would have preferred to fly over the sea, but now their route meant flying overland. They settled at the altitude that gave the best balance between lessened air resistance and sufficient oxygen. Cruising at 15,000 feet had its own dangers. The temperature up there was below freezing, and only the superb insulating qualities of their down feathers kept them warm. Demon winds sometimes sprang up from nowhere to harass them, hurricanes that could deflect them hundreds of miles off course. When that happened, the squadron leader's knowledge of land-marks became crucial.

His father had started a slow descent. He realized they had crossed Australia, from south to north, and were ap-proaching land's end; he recognized the Cape York Penin-sula dead ahead. He could smell the sea beyond it. He could have guided the flock there himself, easily enough, all the way from the Bass Strait. His time would come, of course, perhaps in another year or so. He was a natural for the job of squadron leader.

They recovered their strength in the wetlands of Cape York. The older birds said that in the dry season the Cape was all burning plains, but that after the rains it became marshland. Other birds came there, too: egrets, herons, plovers, sandpipers, and of course the ducks and the geese. Reptiles preyed on them, snakes and crocodiles, but that was the way of it. He knew the estuarine croc, the "saltie." Just as comfortable in salt water as in fresh, it would swim upriver one day and out to sea the next, so that he had to be careful when diving for fish. Around here he had once spotted a saltie out where the sea was deep and blue, a hundred miles from land.

They never tarried in Cape York; a couple of days, just enough to regain normal body weight, no more.

Across the Torres Strait to the land of the Papuas, past the Halhameras, on to Sulawesi, and then the Philippine archipelago, to that one little island with a good stretch of tidal flats. His flock always stopped there. Many other birds knew that island, too. They could expect plenty of company when they arrived.

The island was called Olanggo. A raised coral reef, it was a part of the Plio-Pleistocene Carcar Formation that had risen from the seafloor, taking millions of years to reach the surface and break through the waves. That part was dry land now.

The southern third of the island was alluvium from the Quaternary period, 920 hectares of tidal flats overlain by calcareous sand from the limestone of the coral. This part, most of which was submerged at high tide, was home to nearly 50 kinds of birds. At certain times of the year a like number of other breeds, including his own, stopped at Olanggo in the course of their migrations, so that the flats knew a total of 97 feathered species. Some of them often sortied to the nearby islands, to Sulpa, Kauhagan, Kamungi, Pangan-an, or the twin islets of Kaubian Daku and Kaubian Diut; to Mactan where ugly giant birds made of metal flew around; to Cebu with its bald mountains—but they all regarded Olanggo as the place to be.

For a rookie like him, Olanggo was hard to find among so many islands. His father of course knew exactly where to find it. Olanggo's bearings, as determined by sun, stars, and a feel for North, were fixed in his father's brain as latitude 10°14'N, longitude 124°03'E, or some such avian equivalent. His father also knew, as only a leader of fliers could know, the islands around Olanggo, and the landmarks that led to it.

When they had passed Mindanao his father led the way between the islands of Cebu and Bohol until Mactan hove into view. Olanggo was next to Mactan, to the east; from the air it looked almost completely submerged, because only its northern half was entirely above water, and the rest of it was wetland. The flats actually comprised only a third of the island but the flock's usual approach, from the south, foreshortened things and made the tidelands more conspicuous than the dry land: a luminous patch of green brighter than the surrounding blue of the sea.

High summer always meant a spell in Olanggo, when azure skies never showed more than a ragged bit of cloud or the occasional jet contrail; when every dawn broke to the raucous sounds of all the birds that had come there, the plovers, curlews, snipes, terns, shearwaters, teals, red-shanks, greenshanks, godwits, dowitchers, egrets, frigate birds, herons, shovelers, tattlers, and many others; when spawning fish made the waters grainy with fingerlings and a shadowy underwater streak might splash up as a manta ray leaping clear out of the water; when he could wheel around for hours in the steady winds of the Camotes Sea or the Bohol Strait or the Hilutungan Channel; when his glide path might bring him tangent to an unpaired female, who might coyly ask if he ever found time to fish with all the lazy gliding he did.

And callow youth that he was, he would answer brusquely, say that he was exercising his wings and im-proving his muscle tone for the final leg of their migra-tion, from Olanggo to Kamchatka and then Siberia, the stop in Hokkaido being optional and resorted to only when the squadron leader thought the laggards were having a hard time. But he remembered his manners in time and introduced himself: "Oh, by the way, I'm Cadibarrawirra-canna." And she flapped her wings twice, though she was gliding quite well and didn't really have to do that, and said:

"My name is Nookoona. Nice to meet you, however."

"Eskimo name, is it? Inuit?"

"Inuit, yes. Chukchi, really. That is where I was hatched, however. In Siberia. In the Chukchi lands."

"Bred in the Bass Strait myself. Hatched in Tasma-nia."

"You have such a long name. What does it mean?"

"I don't know. It's just a name."

He taught her how to glide in and out of the two layers of wind. Twice or thrice she had to flap her wings when she nearly stalled, but she turned out to be a fast learner.

"Fly in my slipstream when we resume the journey?"

"Oh, do you mean that? I would really like it, however. You are flying alpha?"

"Delta. Move up to gamma, beta, and alpha in turn. I've yet to qualify on that route, you know."

"You have not been to Siberia before? You look strong enough to lead the squadron, however."

"Been there twice before, but never was too keen on memorizing the landmarks. Truth to tell, I often daydream on the wing. But you know the way there quite well, don't you?"

"I was born there, however. For me, it is like going home."

He spotted a fish near the surface and peeled off in a power dive, pulling out just above the surface to hit the water cleanly and scoop the fish up in his beak. When he rejoined the young female, she suddenly broke off and flew landwards. He followed her. She landed on a stretch of sand, very gracefully, and he barreled in beside her. He offered her the fish. She took it, and in one smooth movement swallowed it headfirst. She restrained a belch, then suddenly seemed to have grown shy. She must have seen it coming, anticipated his question.

"Nookoona," he began, "will you..."

But she had lurched off and taken to the air. She flew only a short hop, landing nearby to join the main congregation of the other seabirds. She melted into the crowd.

He flew off again and began looking for another fish, this time for his own meal. He had memorized her markings, her body odor, and her voice. He could find her again any time he wanted. He didn't know why the Chukchis said "however" all the time, but it wouldn't get on his nerves if he didn't listen to it too much.

He spotted a fish, dived for it, and carried it off to a rock to eat it. He paused a moment, thanking the fishes. He felt strong, very strong. He was fully alert, and could scramble aloft in seconds should the squadron leader squawk the call. He felt he could fly nonstop to Siberia. This time he would observe the landmarks carefully. One more flight, and he could be a squadron leader himself.

Her eyes were on him. He didn't know where she was exactly, but she had to be in that huddle of birds nearby. She was watching him. He could feel her presence across that distance.

He couldn't shake off the timbre of her words. She had a resonant voice, and it seemed to linger in his ear, to echo inside his head. If both of them had a sense for North and for polarized light, how keen were their other instincts? How likely were they to hear each other's thoughts? He supposed he would ask her to be his mate. Would she consent? What would she say? He could almost hear her: *In Siberia I'll lay an egg for you, however.* Or something like that. And if she sounded like she meant it, what could he tell her?

We could take turns sitting on it.

*For two months.*

Until it hatches, and we have a chick to feed...

*Yes, to feed, to teach how to fly and catch fish and navigate...however.*


Cadibarrawirracanna preened his feathers. He spread one wing to its full span. He poked his beak into the oil gland near his tail and oiled his primaries.

The bright sunlight brought out the sheen of his plumage. He basked in the glow of one anointed.

# Fatal Augury

Almost half a century after he died, Don Pepe was trans
ferred from Cebu City to Mandaue. Now his  bones
lay beside those of his eldest son and the latter's wife. That
the father should be brought to the son was of course one
of death's small ironies; in Biblical stories it was always
the other way around, so that the son rested with his fathers. Thus Jacob, dispensing deathbed blessings, also
charged his sons not to bury him in Egypt. Thus Joseph,
embalmed like a pharaoh, called out from the grave, as it
were, to have his bones brought home by Moses.

Mandaue was irony's choice, not Don Pepe's, who had
never lived there. The removal to Mandaue, a few miles
north of where he had been, did not bring him any closer
to Manila, where he had buried his first wife. And it only
increased the distance to his second wife, buried in another cemetery in Cebu City. The Osmeña Cemetery however, in a part of town that was not what it used to be, was
no longer the best place for him. He had lain there, all
alone, for 46 years, remembered mostly by his second wife's
extended family. Not his blood kin, his second marriage
having been without issue, they came every year on All
Souls' Day, with a regularity his own progeny could not

always manage. They honored his memory with offerings of food. In addition to the usual Chinese delicacies they brought him, knowing his tastes, mangoes and oranges, apples and bananas, French bread and real butter, ham and *leche flan*. This sumptuous repast took up all the space atop his crypt, which was about half the size of a regular one. Some of the young relatives, arguing about it, thought he had been a midget. Or perhaps, suggested the one whose mother had fled Nanking in 1937, the Japanese had cut off his legs before beheading him. These wild stories, not rooted in fact, persisted for years. The truth turned out to be quite prosaic. Don Pepe had died of a heart attack. It came without warning, that January of 1944, up there in the mountains of Cebu. Old men and young boys, all that the war could spare, dug his grave. His widow buried him with a minimum of ceremony, ungraced by a priest, in a coffin of cloth and bark. After the war she had him dug up, just a mass of bones now, and then inhumed in the Osmeña Cemetery. This time several priests attended. An orator delivered a eulogy. Later that year, 1946, she too died, and was buried beside her parents in the Carreta Cemetery, half a mile away from her husband.

In 1991 Don Pepe's youngest daughter, Remedios Basa, came home for a visit. A spinster, she was a nurse in a New York City hospital, had taken American citizenship, and wasn't sure which country she would retire to. The condition of her father's tomb appalled her. Most of the roof had been stolen, sheet by sheet. Squatters from nearby apparently found the nooks and crannies near the crypt convenient in the performance of certain of their bodily functions. The place stank.

Medy Basa, as feisty a Basa woman as they come, acquired the necessary permits and arranged everything. It was late September, too early for the Chinese relatives to come spruce the place up and lay out their fine feast. Still, a daughter had more rights than relatives by affinity, and this one moved with the pace of a New Yorker. On All Saints' Day Don Pepe did without his ham and *leche flan*. He was in the Mandaue Cemetery now, where his lineal descendants honored him with flowers and candles. Red wax dripped down his tombstone, the same one his widow had obtained for him in 1946.

*Capitán José M. Basa*

*Nacido de 16 de abril de 1881*

*Fallecio de 19 de enero de 1944*

*Rogad por el*

"Boy, sure startles me every time I see it," Joe Basa said. "My own name on a tombstone."

"That name's a family heirloom, isn't it?" I asked.

"More like a hand-me-down. I'm the fifth José Basa in this family and there must be more of us. There's that Joseph Basa in Dumaguete, second cousin or something of mine. He's Director of the Silliman University Concert Band. I hear they play pretty good. There's Joseph Anthony Basa right here in Mandaue, you know him as Chiquito, second-degree nephew of mine. On the distaff side, there's my cousin Josefina Basa. I don't know about the Basas of Manila, Cavíte and Davao. I expect they've produced their own José Basas."

Joe was José Basa y Vasquez. His father, Francisco Basa y Constantino, was Don Pepe's youngest son. I knew Joe had another namesake cousin, José Basa y Lugay, nicknamed Joselito after a Spanish bullfighter. Lito was a doctor who had migrated to the US in 1975. None of these men wrote their names in full the Spanish way, not anymore. Don Pepe was Capt. José M. Basa. Lito was Dr. Jose L. Basa and didn't even care for the accent over the *e*. Joe was Engr. Jose V. Basa. The middle initial decided everything; without it there was no individuality . I had visions of Basa men, successive generations of them, selecting wives on the basis of appropriate surnames. They would then produce sons to be named José Basa, each with a distinctive middle initial, until they had used up the whole alphabet.

Midnight was an hour away. Soon All Saints' Day would turn into All Souls' Day. My cousins were drinking rum and swapping tall stories at our grandparents' graves, which had the old Mandaue names of Perez and Mendoza. I had left them and walked over to the graves of the Basa family, where I thought I had spotted a guy I hadn't seen in years. I had known Joe Basa in college and I knew the Mandaue Basas were his cousins, but I wasn't sure it was him I had seen earlier. He lived in Cebu City, in the San Nicolas district, and as far as I knew usually visited the Vasquez dead at the Cebu Memorial Park.

"Hey, Joe," I had said, "what's a guy from San Nicolas doing here? Lost your way or something?"

"We just transferred my grandfather," Joe said, "so I thought I'd come here for a change." He grinned, flashing white teeth that seemed to reflect the alabaster of the tombs. "They say people here smash bottles all over the tombs when they're drunk. Must be a lot of fun."

Capt. José M. Basa's tomb was beside his eldest son's. The latter's tombstone had two names: Capt. Antonio C.

Basa, 1902-1974, and Soledad Lugay vda. de Basa, 1906-1989.

I had been out of town then, but I had heard about that 1989 burial. They had exhumed Don Toñing and put him in, just a bag of bones now after 15 years, with Doña Soling in her coffin.

"Let's get drunk," Joe said, producing a bottle of brandy and two snifters, "the better to get you into a throwing mood."

The place was full of Mandaue Basas, Joe's cousins and nephews, mostly drinking beer.

"Let's get rip-roaring drunk," Joe said as he poured, "and fall into the sleep of the dead."

"Or," I said, "until we wake the dead."

"Yes, that's what I meant," Joe said, raising his glass. "To my namesake of a grandfather, mariner, navigator, poet, last of the red-hot lovers."

I choked on my drink. Coughing, I felt the neat brandy sting my throat, then explode into warmth in the pit of my stomach.

"Don't waste it," Joe said. "That's good Fundador."

"Just what they used to drink, right?"

"How did you know? Actually, my namesake used to drink amontillado. Comes from Jerez, same place where Pedro Domecq makes Fundador."

"You've got to tell me more about him," I said.

"Who, Pedro Domecq?"

"No, your grandfather. What's this about a red-hot lover?"

"Oh, that. Sure, I'll tell you. Now, some of it sounds like bull, so I'll throw in a lot of crap. You won't know the difference."

"Forget it," I said. Joe's nephews were getting into a heated argument about PBA teams, and I wanted to join them. But I couldn't leave the bottle unfinished. I was Joe's captive audience. I was trapped.

Counting on his fingers, Joe told me that the first José Basa was the grandfather of his grandfather. Put another way, Joe was a fifth-generation José Basa. This first José Basa was born in San Roque, Cavíte, in 1799 and died in Manila in 1864. His parents were Juar Baza, of Basque and Portuguese extraction, and Juana dela Cruz, a *chinita* beauty whose large bewitching eyes must have come from some fierce Sepoy forebear. Juar's distinctive given name was never confused for "Juan", although in the Binondo of the 17th century Baza soon became Basa. The Basas who remained in Cavíte took another century to adopt the new orthography. Both these branches claimed descent from a common ancestor named Juan Basa, the rajah of Taguig in Soliman's time, a warrior who did his share in fighting Sauzedo and de Goiti.

In 1830 José Basa *primero* married Alfonza Gutiérrez, who bore him Matías, Antonio and Lutgarda before dying of consumption in 1836. José Basa married again early in 1839 and this second wife, Joaquina de San Agustín, brought forth José María that December and then Pio María, Francisco María and María Feliciana at two-year intervals.

The second José Basa, who always used the middle name his pious mother gave all her sons, was the famous one.

Exiled after the Cavíte Mutiny of 1872, he was the one
mentioned in the history footnotes, the one for whom the
streets were named. These J.M. Basa Streets were all over
the country. Davao had one, as did Iloilo. La Carlota in
Negros Occidental had one, and so did the town of Capiz
in Aklan. Mandaue had one, a short street connecting two
long streets, so that nobody could recall which one it was.
Cebu City had one, in the San Nicolas district, connecting
B. Aranas and Tupas Streets. Manila remembered one of
her own, of course. Since all the streets in his birthplace,
Binondo, already had names, the honor went to one in
nearby Tondo. Short and inconspicuous, J.M. Basa Street
was little more than an appendage of Dagupan Street near
the Tutuban Railway Station.

It was José María Basa's elder half-brother, Antonio,
who produced the third José Basa. Antonio Basa y
Gutiérrez, *el doctór homeopatico*, had devoted himself to his
profession, sparing no thought for marriage until the right
woman came along. Basa *el doctor* was past forty when he
found Anselma Mañalac. When their first son was born in
1881 Don Antonio, displaying admirable filial devotion
17 years after his father's death, took his sire's name and
bestowed it on his offspring. José María Basa was thus
named for his dead grandfather, not his exiled uncle. As
Don Toñing put it, the boy's namesake was his grandfather; his uncle was his homonym. Doña Anselma, however, was anxious that her son also bear her family's name.
Accordingly, the boy was taught to write his name as José
Ma. Basa, the abbreviation serving equally well for María
as for Mañalac. This greatly amused José María Basa the
uncle when he visited Manila in 1888; *he* always wrote his
names in full.

For José Ma. Basa, born in 1881, the grandfather who died in 1864 was not much more than a tombstone he saw every *día de todos los santos* at the Paco Cemetery. When he was a small boy just learning to read, he always found himself checking the years of birth and death to make sure the name was his grandfather's, not his. The mind knew, but the eye always got a shock at its recognition of his own name.

As for his grandmother, there hung a portrait of Alfonza Gutiérrez de Basa in the living room, but it was hard to think of this young, very pretty woman as his *lola*. She had died at 25 and his father Antonio, only three at that time, couldn't remember her himself. Anyway, grandmothers were supposed to be old women, like his Lola Joaquina.

In his later years, when people asked him if all those J.M. Basa Streets were named after him, he always said no, it was the other way around; he was named after those streets. It was a bit more involved than that, but he was a man of few words.

As a student at the Ateneo de Manila in the nineties, José Ma. Basa took to abbreviating his middle name the old Spanish way, capital $M$ and raised minuscule $a$, no period: José M$^a$ Basa. He reverted to the punctuated form when a Jesuit priest chided him for the affectation. In the American period he was to switch to the Anglo custom and use only a middle initial: José M. Basa. However, he would not go as far as pronouncing the "M." as one syllable; it was always "emme," two syllables or nothing. By this time he had attained the rank of Captain in the merchant marine and could prefix his name with that title. It was a way of coming out of the shadow of his homonym. His uncle was a businessman who had been the manager, at twenty (in 1860), of a distillery in Trozo. In Hongkong too the man's business acumen afforded him a fairly good living. The nephew followed the main family tradition and became a mariner. Becoming a captain was merely what the family expected of him. Baza men from Cavíte had been shipwrights and seafarers as far back as anyone could recall. Baza men had helped build the first Acapulco galleons; Baza men had sailed in those galleons back and forth across the Pacific, or gone down in them to the seafloor.

There remained other homonyms. His cousin José María Basa y Panlaque, Hongkong's gain if not necessarily Manila's loss, wrote his name as José María Basa, *hijo*. Sometimes he wrote it as José María Basa, *fils*, or as José María Basa, *l.j.* (*le jeune*). To his credit, he never wrote it as José María Basa, Jr.

There was the Cavíte lawyer José Baza, born 1843, the son of shipwright Francisco Baza (not the brother of Pio and Feliciana) and Felipa Enriques. Spanish usage, with a will of its own, caused two letters to exchange places and by 1872 he had become José Basa y Enríquez. He too had been exiled that year; his name too was in a few history footnotes. José Basa y Enríquez came home from exile after three years and went on to represent Cavíte, together with Hugo Ilagan, in the 1898 Malolos Congress.

During José Ma. Basa's childhood the story of the three Basa men exiled in 1872 was told and retold in the family countless times. He knew it by heart.

The brothers José María and Pio María Basa y San Agustín, and their Cavíte kinsman José Basa y Enríquez, were members of a secret society, the *Comité de Reformadores*, formed in late 1868 after the Glorious September Revolution in Peninsular Spain. In 1869 they were among those who serenaded the liberal Governor-General, Carlos María dela Torre. In 1870 an article written by José María Basa was published in Madrid, in the periodical *El Eco Filipino*. It argued for the secularization of parishes in Las Islas Filipinas. In 1871 Rafael Izquierdo replaced dela Torre as Governor-General, and under this tyrant the Cavíte Mutiny broke out in January of 1872. Fort Santiago filled up with arrested men. The priests Burgos, Gómez and Zamora were garroted.

They were not the only ones executed. Thirteen military men were shot, nine in Bagumbayan and four in Cavíte. Twenty-nine men died while in detention, probably under torture. Some 149 men were exiled, 80 to Zamboanga, a few each to Davao, Balabac, and Paragua Island, and some to Spain. The most dangerous ones were sent to the Mariana Islands.

The three Basa men were among those taken from Fort Santiago in March of 1872 and put aboard the ship *Flores de Mayo* for Guam. Of the 22 *deportados*, ten were priests, and one a woman. The men included Joaquin Pardo de Tavera, Maximo Paterno, Gervasio Sánchez—most of the *jaranistas* of 1869 were accounted for. Among the priests were Pedro Dandan, Jose Guevarra, and Vicente del Rosario. The woman, Doña Gertrudis Gorricho Pardo de Tavera, was Don Joaquin's wife—the only wife permitted to accompany her husband into exile.

Two of the Basas remained in Guam until 1875, when conditional pardon was granted. José María Basa y San Agustín escaped in May of 1874, together with Balbino Mauricio and Antonio María Regidor. They dressed themselves up as priests, poetic justice for Basa, who loathed the Spanish friars, and got away on an American whaling ship, the four-masted schooner *Rupax*. Its captain,

Holcomb, was sympathetic to them. The *Rupax* took them to Yap Island, which however was still Spanish territory.

The first ship out of Yap was an English steamer, the *Pelican*. Depending on who told the story, they either paid for their passage in Yap money, stone disks the size of *carruaje* wheels, or in Mexican silver pesos. The *Pelican* took them south of the equator to the Solomon Islands, which were British.

In Punta Cruz on Guadalcanal they contracted for passage on an outrigger, actually two outrigger canoes lashed together. The Solomon Islanders, who navigated by traditional methods, kept them waiting until the monsoon winds changed. They left in September with the southwest monsoon and got off at Peleliu in the Pelew group, sunburnt and possessed of good sea legs after a month and a half under sail.

Two months passed in idyllic splendor, then they made their way to Koror in time to catch a German merchant vessel, the *Pomerania*, for Hongkong. The captain, a Prussian Junker, charged them exorbitant fares and spent most of the trip talking to them about his fellow Junker, von Bismarck, and the war concluded three years previously, in 1871. He was glad that Elsass-Lothringen had been liberated from the Gauls. Basa, who felt it was the French who had lost Alsace-Lorraine to the Second Reich, held his tongue.

Basa was granted political asylum in Hongkong. The other two went on to Europe, Mauricio settling in Madrid and Regidor becoming a lawyer in London.

Even after the pardon granted in 1875, and the amnesty in 1876, Basa declined to come home. Life in a country owned by friars was not for him. He visited Manila but twice, first in 1888 and again in 1897. In Hongkong the spacious Basa residence on N° 7 Remedios Terrace, Arbuthnot Road, near the Zoölogical and Botanical Gardens, became a haven for compatriots passing through in the eighties and nineties. José Ma. Basa y Mañalac stayed there with his uncle for two years at the end of the century. He was eighteen that memorable year of 1899; his uncle was going on sixty. The Americans were making war, and Manila was no place for college studies. He took up the study of law at the Hongkong Technical Institute, which had not yet become the University of Hongkong. José María Basa y San Agustín often regaled his young homonym of a nephew with stories of the men who had stayed in that very house. Don Pepe, as everyone called him, seemed to regain something of his lost youth when telling these stories. He had acquired an air of moroseness, or so his daughters said, after becoming a widower in 1890. His wife Bernarda, *née* Panlaque, by whom he had eight children, had stayed in Manila after their 1888 visit. The next two years passed all too quickly; Tio Pepe had been unable to attend her funeral. He had been caught up in the propaganda movement. He told his nephew stories about Marcelo Hilario del Pilar, Mariano Ponce, and Graciano Lopez-Jaena whose Ilonggo accent he always found most charming. José Protacio Rizal Mercado y Alonso, who was also called Don Pepe, went there too, the first time in 1888. In 1889 *La Solidaridad* began coming out from Barcelona, and Basa helped smuggle it into Manila.

He became quite a smuggler. A Cavíte kinsman of his, Román Basa, was a *segundo oficial* at the *Comandancia General de Manila*. Román Basa knew the *maquinista* of the ship *San Juan*, which plied the Manila-Hongkong run.

José María Basa, through business agents, would send a consignment of liquors and spirits, in *demijuanas*, to Manila. The Caviteño *maquinista* would tell Román Basa which demijohns contained printed matter. It was up to Román Basa to get these past customs.

It turned out to be a good system. At first they sent only minor works in the demijohns. As José María Basa grew bolder he sent pamphlets he had written himself, under the pen name Kulog, which was the Tagalog word for "thunder." In March of 1888, for example, he sent his tract *"Viva España. Viva el Rey. Viva el ejército. Fuera los frailes."* The following month he sent his *proclama* entitled *"Escándaloso, horrendo, y punible delito perpetrado en el Monasterio de Santa Clara por un Fraile Franciscano."* which was an account of an incident that took place in 1883. Later, he found that Rizal had drawn on the same story for the closing scene of the *Noli Me Tangere*.

The *Noli* went in the demijohns, too. That was in 1888. That was also the year Balbino Mauricio came over from Madrid for a short visit. It had been thirteen years since their great escape from Guam. The two of them, Basa and Mauricio, recounted their adventure over and over, sometimes pressing Rizal into Regidor's role, until Rizal, thoroughly bored, suggested they go someplace for a trip. The three of them went to Macao to visit Francisco Lécaroz, the last Filipino delegate to the Spanish Cortes. The Spanish consul in Hongkong, who kept *indios bravos* under surveillance, sent a watchdog to accompany them. It was an *insulare* Rizal had known casually in Manila, a Señor Saenz de Baranda.

His Tio Pepe was proud of the epithet bestowed by Marcelo del Pilar, *corresponsal nato en esa colonia*. He was proud of his success in smuggling the *Noli* into Manila.

Rizal had to write him in 1889, asking him to stop. They were getting so many copies that hiding them was becoming a problem. It was endangering the safety of some people.

José Ma. Basa remembered those novels. He was eight when the *guardia civil* raided the house. Finding nothing, for Antonio Basa *el doctor* had hidden the family's copies well, they went on to his eldest uncle's house. Still finding nothing there, they held Matías Basa on some pretext, throwing him into Fort Santiago's dank, underground *bartolina* and keeping him there for a month.

José Ma. Basa was twelve when the family acquired copies of the *Fili* and thirteen when he was allowed to read it, and the *Noli*, too. His father and uncles debated the merits of both novels incessantly, and soon they were soliciting his views, too.

His Tio Pepe told him about the Liga Filipina. It had been his original idea, and he had prevailed on Rizal to write its constitution and by-laws. This was a sort of avuncular deference to Rizal's talents and high standing. Rizal, the younger man by 22 years, was much like a special nephew to his Tio Pepe. As for José Ma. Basa, already the nephew in this situation, it seemed natural to think of Pepe Rizal, 20 years his senior, as another Tio Pepe.

His uncle had sent Rizal in Ghent, Belgium, some money. This was in 1891, when Rizal was printing the *Fili*. Rizal soon sent him the first copy. Sixto Lopez got the second copy. Valentin Ventura, whose money came at the most critical moment, got the third copy and the original manuscript. That same year, when Rizal left Europe for the last time, the money for his boat fare from Marseilles to Hongkong was lent him by Tio Pepe.

The last time Tio Pepe saw Rizal was in 1892. Rizal had hung out his doctor's shingle at nearby d'Aguilar Street, 5, N° 2 Rednaxela Terrace. Rizal printed his business cards in English on one side and Chinese on the other...

Tio Pepe remembered Josephine Leopoldine Taufer, too. She had stayed at the house for a few days in 1897. As Rizal's widow, she asked for the books Rizal had left for safekeeping there. They filled three bookcases and were worth, at a conservative estimate, HK$3,000—a tidy sum. His Tio Pepe asked Miss Taufer, better known as Josephine Bracken, for proof of marriage. Bracken, who could not have been more than 20, showed him a book Rizal had given her, *Imitación de Cristo* por Thomas à Kempis. On the flyleaf was an inscription in English: *"To my dear and unhappy wife Josephine—José Rizal 30 December 1896"*. His Tio Pepe was touched, but needed legal proof. He suggested that Bracken write to the British Consulate in Manila for a copy of the marriage certificate. Bracken, however never produced that certificate. The books stayed. And were still there. Would he like to see them?

Years later, he learned that his uncle had turned them over to the Mercado-Rizal family in 1902.

The stories amplified and refined his image of Rizal. He had seen the man only once, with the eyes of a boy, but everything remained vivid in his mind. He stared into the distance, no longer listening to his uncle prate on, and then it came back to him.

Early in the chilly dawn. He stands as close to Don Pepe as he can, as far front as he dares, just off the line of fire.

Don Pepe, arms loosely bound elbow to elbow at his back, faces Manila Bay. From his right hand dangle the beads of a rosary, its silver crucifix contrasting sharply with his black coat. With him are three Spaniards, two in black *soutanes* and the third in a military uniform. Behind them is the firing squad, eight native troopers in front of eight Spanish soldiers.

The crowd has grown larger. The three girls next to José Ma. Basa have been pushed closer to him. His eyes meet those of the nearest one and she asks him,

*"Anong uri ang dala nilang sandata?"*

It surprises him, because upperclass girls speak only Spanish and love to feign ignorance of the Tagalog language. But he halfturns with all the aplomb of his fifteen years and quietly replies:

"Remington muskets. And those Spaniards behind them have Mauser rifles."

His voice sounds funny to his own ears. His Tagalog betrays a Spanish accent, and it embarrasses him.

*"¿Dos clases de armas,* to shoot just one man?"

"Only the Macabebes will shoot him," he tells her. *"Kung hindi nila maatim*, that's when the Spanish soldiers will shoot *them*."

*"¡Que horrible!"*

"They say one of the Remingtons is loaded with a blank. Each man can convince himself it wasn't his gun that fired the fatal bullet. That it was the other seven."

The soldiers' mascot, a white dog with brown spots, seems to him a very beautiful animal. In the crisp predawn air time itself seems to be standing still, with everything happening very slowly, very clearly. Don Pepe, with a shake of his head, declines a blindfold proffered by one of the Jesuit priests, then addresses the captain of the guard. José Ma. Basa, looking on intently, is all ears. The chatter of the girls distracts him. He strains to make out the words between the condemned man and the captain, even as he attempts to read their lips.

*"No puede ser,"* the captain is saying, *"porque tengo órdenes de fusilarle por la espalda."*

Don Pepe argues, with some heat, *"Yo no he sido traidor a mi patria ni a la nación española."*

The captain looks down from his full height.

*"Mi deber es cumplir las órdenes que he recibido."*

Don Pepe snorts.

*"Pues bien, fusíleme como quiera."*

Don Pepe turns to shake hands with the Spanish officer beside him. Hampered as he is by his bound elbows, the gesture is rather awkward.

"That's Taviel de Andrade, isn't it?" asks one of the girls.

"Yes," replies José Ma. Basa, "that's Teniente Luis."

Don Pepe's military defender during the trial, he might have added. Brother to Teniente José, who had been Don Pepe's bodyguard in Calamba in 1888. But he supposes the girls know all that.

A doctor feels Don Pepe's pulse.

Then everyone has moved back, Don Pepe has faced forward and missed seeing one of the priests start to bless him, the roll of the drums seems to last forever, the troopers are taking aim.

*"Consummatum est!"* shouts Don Pepe.

Crack of musketfire shattering the stillness. Startled birds taking to the air. Beyond the distant mountains, the sun about to break. Don Pepe crumbles ever so slowly and then, incredibly, wrenches around and spins on his heel so that he falls supine.

Fallen, Don Pepe lies face up, eyes still open. First to run to him is the spotted dog. It whimpers piteously, sniffs the body, recoils, and then scampers off in circles. Counterclockwise, notes José Ma. Basa in a curiously detached way, recalling some lesson about the Coriolis effect. The captain of the guard trots forward, gives the *coup de grâce*. A shot in the heart.

"*¡Viva España!*" he cries, arms high in the air. The Spaniards in the crowd all echo him.

"*¡Viva España!*"

Raising that cry is customary, but now the captain adds another exhortation.

"*¡Mueran los traidores!*" he booms.

"*¡Mueran los traidores!*"

The captain shouts it twice more, and each time is answered by his compatriots:

"*¡Viva España! ¡Mueran los traidores!*"

One of the Jesuits kneels by the dead body and gently closes the eyes. Don Pepe's sisters come forward, pleading to soak their handkerchiefs in the blood. The captain waves them off. José Ma. Basa turns away and heads home, at a stunned walk at first, then breaking into a run. In the east, the sky bleeds red.

Fighting men could be seen in the Gardens. They carried no weapons, but they were a force that soon erupted into the Boxer Rebellion of 1900. Riots broke out in the streets. It was the end of José Ma. Basa's studies in Hongkong. His uncle advised him to return to Manila. The Americans were winning and would soon take over the country. Not necessarily a bad thing. They had once discussed this, he and Rizal: What if?

What if Spain were forced out of the Islands? A power vacuum, they agreed, would be created. Who would rush in to fill it? No, not Britain. Not France. Not Germany nor Holland. Only the Estados Unidos.

In his 1889 essay *"Filipinas dentro de cien años"* Rizal elaborated on the ideas developed in that discussion. He suggested that "...the great American Republic...whose interests lie in the Pacific...may someday dream of foreign possession."

Radical as this idea might have seemed then, Rizal thought it unlikely of the USA, "...as this is contrary to her traditions." And that was as far as Rizal went.

Basa went much further. He tended to lump the British and the Americans together, Nordic peoples separated only by a common language, and perhaps his prosperity on a barren island that had flourished under the Union Jack had influenced his thinking. He wrote two manifestoes favoring cooperation with the Estados Unidos. In his scenario the Islands would have autonomous government for five years, be a US protectorate for another five, then be granted final and absolute independence.

In May of 1898 Basa had feared that the Treaty of Paris might cede the Islands back to Spain. Together with Doroteo Cortés and A.G. Medina, he petitioned for annexation of the Islands by the USA. This petition they coursed through the US consul in Hongkong.

"A silly thing to do," José María Basa y San Agustín told his nephew. "Naïve. We didn't know better then."

Late in 1898, after Christmas, President McKinley issued his "Benevolent Assimilation" proclamation. In Manila, early in 1899, General Elwell S. Otis published the text after editing it and inserting some amendments. Otis replaced such words as "sovereignty", "protection" and "right of cession" with softer terms. In Iloilo however, General Marcus P. Miller published McKinley's original text. With that, the cat was out of the bag.

General Antonio Luna, in his newspaper *La Independencia*, wrote a fierce condemnation of McKinley's imperialism. General Emilio Aguinaldo, as President of the Revolutionary Government, issued a counter-proclamation, denouncing American intrusion on the sovereignty of the Islands. Two weeks later the Malolos Republic was inaugurated and another couple of weeks after that the Philippine-American War had begun.

"When Miller published that original text," Don Pepe told his homonym, "I experienced what the French call *presque vu*, or 'so nearly seen' as we might say it. Pluperfect vision, in other words.

"Suddenly, I knew things were not what they might have seemed to me. In a single flash of intuition, I knew the Americans wanted our Islands. Not for any altruistic motives, but for selfish ones."

He paused, took a sip of cognac.

"Miller's act may have been inadvertent, but it seemed to me the fatal augury."

The strange turn of phrase resonated in José Ma. Basa's mind. He was to brood on it for years. What had his uncle meant? His uncle had not said "ill omen" or "evil portent" (*mal aguero, presagio*). He had not said *presentimiento* or *corazonado*. He had said *fatal augurio*. What did that mean?

Gremlins haunted his mind. The phrase had ignited his imagination and lit up a memory he thought he had exorcised. He was 16 again. He knew the passwords were "anak ng bayan" for a *katipon*, "Gom-Bur-Za" for a *kawal*, and "Rizal" for a *bayani*. Still, he could not get in. And so he asked his father's cousin Román to help him. He was not sure what degree of cousin to his father this Tio Román was. The man's parents were Mariano Basa the Cavíte *pukot* operator and Dorotea Estéban. A pukot was a deep-sea fishing net: this branch of the family had combined the nautical tradition with the entrepreneurial. Román Basa was then some 47 years of age. His Katipunan alias was "Liwanag."

After the usual niceties, Román Basa told him to get on with his studies. What was he going to take up? He could earn a *bachiller en filosofía* degree at the Universidad de Santo Tomás in Intramúros. That was what his namesake had done, wasn't it? Then he could go into business, manage a distillery in Trozo or something. Or he could follow in the footsteps of that other namesake of his, take up law and ultimately run for public office...

"Tio Román, I want to join the Katipunan."

"No. Out of the question. You're too young. Think of your future."

"I am thinking of my future. Won't you help me? Surely a word from the President..."

"*Hijo*, that was four years ago. I was President for only a year. I withdrew in 1894. Don't you see? I have no influence whatsoever now. Not since Bonifacio and I dis-agreed about a few things."

"What about?"

"Simplified initiation rites, for one thing. He insists on those tedious rites of his. Rather silly, actually."

"And just for that..."

"No, not just that. There was the issue of money, too. The root of all evil, indeed. I told him the Katipunan was spending too lavishly. I told him to his face he couldn't spend KKK funds like that, it all came from the lifeblood of the people, it stood for a lot of sacrifice on their part and should be held sacred..."

Román Basa's fist pounded the table.

"You know our family's attitude to money," Román Basa went on. "We've always been above reproach where it's concerned. I had that point of honor to consider. But the last straw was when he insisted that Lucio be initiated. He's always wanted Lucio to join. I was willing to give what I could, but not my own son. Let Lucio join of his own volition, not through coercion."

"So who's President now?"

"Bonifacio himself."

"The second President."

"No, he's the third. Deodato Arellano was the first. He and I lasted about a year each. Both of us thought we were to play active roles. I even created a women's sec-tion. But each of us soon found out we were meant to be figureheads, nothing more."

"You're out of it entirely now?"

"Well, if it comes to war, I shall heed the call."

"Whose call?"

Román Basa sighed.

"You know, the Society is breaking up in two. Bonifacio now leads what they call the Magdiwang faction. Most of my friends are in the other faction, the Magdalo. I've preferred not to join them. It's Bonifacio's movement, after all. He started it. I would like to see him fulfill its aims."

"You don't question his fitness to lead the Katipunan? I've heard that men like Tirona and the Aguinaldos do."

"No, I don't. Bonifacio's heart is in the right place. It's just that he's from a poor family and all this money and attention seem to have gone to his head. It's distracting him from the real issues. But I think that when the crisis comes, he'll get back to his ideals."

"And you, Tio Román? You'll join the Magdalo?"

"I don't know, *hijo*. Maybe I'll go back to the *pukot*."

He remembered not so much the actual words as the aroma from his kinsman's cigar. An Alhambra Corona. Then his memory, unbidden, supplied the next image, and Román Basa stands again at Bagumbayan, dressed in his formal whites, with hat and cane, one morning in February 1897, just before sunrise.

Musketfire shatters the stillness. Birds take to the air. Slowly the six men crumple to the ground. Román Basa is the last to stop twitching.

He had seen it in advance, the day of their conversation. Something in the man's demeanor, in his very tone of voice, the way he pounded the table with his fist, had foreshadowed his martyrdom. Had augured ill. Was it another example? Was this what his Tio Pepe had meant?

He did not dwell too long on morbid thoughts. He was too young, as his Tio Román had said. There was school to go back to. Should he continue his law studies? But now it would mean American law. Not so bad in theory; he admired their system of trial by a jury of peers, for one. However, none of the universities in Manila would credit his two years at the Hongkong Technical Institute. If he had to begin all over again, it might as well be something that took heed of the call of the sea.

In July of 1901 José Ma. Basa was one of 83 pupils who began studies at the Nautical Academy of Manila. The Americans had taken over: the superintendent was Lt. (s.g.) George F. Cooper, USN, and there were five instructors, all men of the US Navy. The subjects were mathematics, history, drawing, mechanics and practical seamanship; the medium of instruction was Spanish. The course was to take three years.

In July Lt. Cooper decreed a few changes: the medium of instruction would be English, and lessons in English grammar and literature were to be added. The course would now be four years long.

English was not too difficult for José Ma. Basa, although he still thought it was a crazy language. Its grammar gave too much freedom, and that was why poets in English wrote such outrageous lines. English also badly needed to reform its spelling.

His English was mediocre, but better than most of his classmates'. He had learned the language in Hongkong, his uncle having encouraged him to study it. José María Basa was fluent in both English and Cantonese, as befitted a longtime resident of Hongkong. José Ma. Basa learned enough of both to get by, but uncle and nephew always conversed in Spanish and Tagalog. José Ma. Basa's ear was attuned to English as spoken by the British in Hongkong. Now, at the Nautical Academy, he found the English his American teachers spoke very jarring. It no longer sounded like a Germanic language. It was a nasal language, and every word had a twang. He had a good ear, and soon could do accurate imitations of his instructors' speeches. In class however, whenever called upon to recite, his English was heavily Spanish-accented, full of florid phrases that sounded like literal translations from a Romance language.

July had been for beginnings, not just of nautical school but also of his courtship of 15-year-old Felisa Constantino. A mere child the last time he saw her, two years before, she had matured early. He had gone to attend Mass at the Quiapo Church, where he and Felisa used to sing with the choir. That was where he had first met her, although it was her elder sister Catalina who had caught his eye then. Now he found that Felisa was the featured soloist. Her voice soared to the vaults of the nave, truly the voice of an angel, and he knew he was hopelessly in love with her. The little girl he remembered was gone; here sang a woman.

Catalina was also being courted, by a young doctor. José Ma. Basa sometimes arrived at the Constantino house at the same time as the other ardent suitor, Dr. José Lugay. Once, after taking their leave of the sisters, the two young Don Pepes went off and engaged in a drinking bout. The nautical student trailed the doctor by eight years in age, but not in toasts.

The girls' parents, Francisco Constantino and Rafaela Sánchez, decided on a double wedding. One fine November morning in 1901 Catalina and Felisa took as their respective husbands the two Josés. The new Lugay couple were 28 and 23, just about the right age for both of them. The Basa couple were 20 and 16. Young love indeed, and perhaps all the more achingly beautiful for that.

While José Ma. Basa returned to his studies, Dr. Lugay was assigned to Guiuan, Samar, by the new American government.

Upon finishing nautical school, José Ma. Basa became a *segundo oficial de cubierto*, or Second Mate, in 1905. He was now the father of Antonio, born 1902, Carolina (1903), Arturo (1905—named after Port Arthur in Manchuria, his way of paying tribute to the Japanese Navy's victory over the combined Russian fleets). His wife Felisa, whom he fondly called Chichang, soon became pregnant again. Between 1901 and 1924 Chichang was to become pregnant an astounding 22 times. Only 11 of these did not end in miscarriage, stillbirth, or a difficult delivery and a blue baby. The eleven survivors included Ernesto, Carmen, Narcisa, Soledad, Rosario, Herminia, Francisco and Remedios. The other eleven, those who went early to Heaven, also had names: Juan, Román, Rafaela, Alfonza...

He named none of his sons José after himself. Not even the ones he baptized himself, those who died before a priest could be summoned.

Kith and kin were uppermost in his considerations when in 1907 José Ma. Basa was called upon to serve as *juez de paz* in Guiuan, Samar. His grades in Law at the Hongkong Technical Institute had been impressive, but he was reluctant to abandon the mariner's life. Chichang however, eager for a reunion with her sister, prevailed upon him to accept the post. She wanted to show her sister her four children, wanted to see Ninay's three.

In Guiuan the kids all became noisy playmates. They chattered happily in Spanish, the Basa children not being disposed to learn Waray, nor the young Lugays Tagalog. Dr. Lugay and Ninay had three children then, all born in Guiuan: José Jr., Rafael, and Soledad. (Later they were to have three more, Luisa, Luis, and Claro.)

When the cousins played games, they would choose an "it" by a counting-out rhyme:

> *Pin pin, serafin*
> *agua ronda peconda*
> *jao jao, carabao*
> *San Miguel arcangel*

They also played leapfrog, for which there was a ditty:

> *A la una, salta la mula*
> *capitán de la guerra.*
> *A las dos, campaña de relos.*
> *A las tres y almires*
> *Cuarta, que te falta,*
> *los mendigos de la cesta.*
> *Quinta, que te pinta...*

Guiuan, as it turned out, had more need of a doctor than a judge. Dr. Lugay became the sort of general practitioner who could diagnose illnesses by sight or feel before the patient had said anything, a country doctor who often accepted payment in kind.

The problem of what to call each other, first encountered in Manila after their double wedding, now recurred. Each was the other's wife's brother-in-law. For the two sisters they were *esposo* and *cuñado*, one or the other. But they themselves were not brothers-in-law. Their wives had urged them to call each other *cuñado*, but that was not right. In Tagalog or Waray they were *bilas*, for which there was no Spanish term.

They settled on *hermano político*. In some way at least, they could call themselves brothers.

The *juez* at 26 must have been thought to be rather young for a magistrate, but then again this did not really matter. José Ma. Basa found the Warays a proud race who were quick to take offense and who could nurse grievances for generations. Most of them were too polite to bother him, preferring to settle accounts according to ancient, unwritten tribal law.

Guiuan was perched on Samar's eastern edge, facing the vast Pacific Ocean. The seafood there was the best they had ever eaten, crabs, prawns and lobsters twice as big as those in Manila, and more kinds of fish in a week than they usually had in a month. They feasted on baked *tipay* on the half shell (seasoned with white pepper; dipped into a sauce of garlic and butter); on *lawot-lawot*; on *dagmay*; on *hinatukan nga bilibol*. They learned how to drink *bahalina*, breaking a couple of raw eggs into the pitcher and pouring in a cupful of seawater. It was as different from Cavíte *tuba* as sherry was different from claret, or whiskey from bourbon, or vodka from ginebra...

"Or *basi* from *pangasi*," Ninay put in.

Manila was in another country, it seemed. Newspapers reached them several days late. The newly elected Philippine Assembly was convening, and all the talk was of who would be elected Speaker. They were all quite sure it would be Pedro Paterno. There was no one who could hold a candle to him: no one like the son of the 1872 exile Mariano Paterno; no one like the negotiator of the pact of Biak-na-Bato; no one like the former President of the Malolos Congress, doctor, poet, novelist.

When the young unknown from Cebú, Sergio Osmeña, was chosen Speaker by acclamation, the news left them dumfounded.

"Why, he's only 29!" exclaimed Dr. Lugay, who was 35.

"My age," said José Ma. Basa, who was actually three years younger. He wondered what his uncle in Hongkong thought of it. José María Basa would surely have rooted for his fellow exile's son. But it was 1907; a new generation had come to the fore.

Love of the outdoors spurring them on, they went horseback riding, the four of them, to the town of Balangiga.

"I've a standing invitation from the parish priest," Dr. Lugay told them, "to visit. I treated him once for some minor ailment."

The priest, Padre Donato Guinbaolibot, took them to the house of the late mayor, *capitán* Pedro Abayon. The mayor's widow, Doña Trining, served them *budbod*, hot chocolate, and ripe mangoes. Talk soon turned to the time the Americans moved in. Guiuan was the first town to be occupied, then Basey. Balangiga lay between these two, so they knew they were next.

"General Vicente Lukban and his guerrillas," Doña Trining told them, "controlled the whole area: Gipordos, Lawaan, Quinapundan…

"Company C of the Ninth Infantry Battalion arrived in August 1901. They were veterans of the Boxer Rebellion in China. Their CO, Captain Thomas Connell, a West Point graduate, was also a veteran of the war in Cuba. Their XO was First Lieutenant Edward Bumpus. They had a surgeon, Major R.S. Griswold.

"They took over the *tribunál,* the *convento,* and two houses nearby, large nipa huts. In charge of one hut was Sergeant Betron and of the other was Sergeant Markley. There were 74 of them all in all, 3 officers and 71 men…we had counted them very carefully.

"They confiscated all the knives, bolos, and bladed implements we had. They ordered us to clean up our surroundings but nobody moved to obey. They then detained eighty of our best able-bodied men, issued them picks, shovels, and *machetes,* and ordered them to clear the underbrush from the población to the edge of the forest. Those machetes and picks had to be returned every evening. Of the 80 men, they crammed 45 into a tent meant for 16.

"My husband hatched plans for a surprise attack on them with his Jefe de Policía, Valeriano Abanador, and one of Lukban's officers, Capitán Eugenio Daza. Abanador had 46 policemen. We could muster some 500 men from the 6th and 7th Commands of Lukban's forces.

"It was decided to attack them on a Sunday morning at breakfast time, seven o'clock. That was the only time the *americanos* left their rifles in their barracks. The 500 men were divided into seven groups of seventy each. Five of these stayed on the town's outskirts, waiting for the signal. The 6th Company, Capitán Daza with men from Lawaan, went as churchgoers to the early morning Mass. It would look strange if the whole congregation was made up of men, so many of them came dressed in women's clothes. As there was to be a *pintakasi* that day, those who came as men brought fighting cocks to church.

"On Thursday Pedro had managed to secure the temporary release of forty of the eighty detained men. He told the CO he needed them for work in the fields. But when he returned them in the afternoon, they were not the same men. He had substituted forty guerrillas for them. The next day, he also exchanged the other forty in the same way.

"On Saturday, two coffins were brought to the church. Inside each was a child who had died of cholera. Hidden in the coffins were knives, *sundang* or bolos.

"On Sunday, September 28, 1901, Abanador led the 7th Company and began cleaning the streets. He had divided his men into three groups, one each for the *municipio,* the *convento,* and the private houses.

"The little boys who go to the belfry to ring the church bells were instructed to watch the Jefe. Abanador would signal them with his cane. When they rang the bells, the attack would break out. Alternatively, Abanador would signal the attack by firing a gun.

"Everything went as planned. Padre Donato said Mass. None of the Americans attended. I don't think there were any Catholics among them. The churchgoers, both men and 'women,' armed themselves with the bolos from the coffins.

"The Mass was ending when Abanador himself approached the sentry. He killed the man with a knife, then waved his cane and yelled "*Yanâ!*—Now!" The boys in the belfry began ringing the churchbells. Abanador picked up the dead sentry's rifle and fired it. The church doors opened and the men rushed out. The streetcleaners whipped out their bolos and stormed the huts of Sergeants Betron and Markley.

"Capitán Daza's men headed for the *convento* and the mess hall tent. They cut the guy ropes and the tent fell in, trapping the Americans inside. Our men hacked at them from outside.

"Abanador and his men stormed the larger hut. They hacked most of the men inside to death before a wounded *americano* corporal found his Colt .45 and fired three times at Abanador. The other men finished off the corporal, but Abanador had been killed instantly.

"Capitán Pedro rushed across the second-floor corridor connecting the church and the convent. They found the three officers inside, and four enlisted men. They killed Lt. Bumpus, Maj. Griswold, and the four other men, who had valiantly shielded their CO from the attack. Capt. Connell, in his pajamas, leaped out the window and ran into the street. Our men overtook him and cut him down. An American on the ground fired at the men on the second floor of the convent, and capitán Pedro was hit..."

"Thirty-six of them were killed outright," said Padre Guinbaolibot. "Half of Company C. The remainder fled in 3 *bancas* and a *baloto*. For our part, we lost 14 of our men, including *capitán* Abayon and *jefe* Abanador, plus two who died of their wounds later."

"But you followed their boats?" prompted Dr. Lugay.

"Yes," said Doña Trining. "The guerrillas of Capitán Daza followed them along the shore. The three bancas with a total of 27 men in them stayed well out to sea. some of those men died of their injuries before they reached Basey the next morning.

"The fourth boat, a baloto with 9 men in it, was easier to follow. None of them really knew how to handle that kind of boat. The guerrillas overtook them off the town of Bulusao and opened fire on them with their own guns, the American rifles they had taken as booty. They killed 7 of them. Two men survived by pretending to be dead under the bodies of their comrades. Those two managed to reach Tolosa.

"Of course, the Americans came back for revenge. Gen. Jacob Smith turned Samar into a howling wilderness.

"Anyone they passed, young, old—they killed. For nine months the slaughter went on. They took no prisoners, not even the old people."

The quiet way she said this made an impression on José Ma. Basa. The Waray language, typically spoken in a singsong accent, had always seemed funny to him. But now it had come forth with words that were to haunt him for a long time:

*"Basta agi-an, bata, tigurang—ginpatay. Siyam ka bulan nga nagpinamatay, waray gikuha nga mga preso, pati mga tigurang."*

"...there was a deserter?" Dr. Lugay was asking.

"Yes," said Padre Guinbaolibot. He deserted well before our surprise attack and fled to the hills. He eventually joined Capitán Daza's unit. His name was Corporal William Denton.

"Two other deserters," said Doña Trining, "came from another company, based in Tacloban. They must have found General Smith's orders too harsh. I don't remember their names. They joined General Lukban's men. The Americans captured those two in 1903. Recaptured, I should say."

"What about Corporal Denton?" asked Dr. Lugay.

"Denton was killed in action in 1902," said Padre Guinbaolibot. "Fighting on our side."

"I still have that rifle the chief of police took from the sentry," Señora Abayon said. She went into a room and came back with it.

"Fifty of these were spirited away by our men, together with 25,000 rounds of ammunition, from the American camp. They put them to good use in the months that followed."

She handed it to Dr. Lugay.

"Krag Jorgensen 30-06," the doctor read, turning the rifle over in his hands.

"Want to test-fire it?" Señora Abayon asked. "And the other guns, too?"

She took out her gun collection, all firearms taken from enemies fallen in battle: a Mauser rifle, an old Remington musket, a shiny new Smith & Wesson .38, complete with tooled leather belt and holster.

They set up a target range in the woods back of the house. The two *hermanos políticos* fired a few rounds each, marveling at the recoil of the Krag. Chichang too fired a shot, as did Ninay after some prodding. Señora Abayon watched them in silence, making no move to fire any of the guns herself. José Ma. Basa picked up the Mauser.

"It lacks a rear sight," he said.

"Yes," Dr. Lugay said. "A compatriot of ours must have removed it after he took this gun from a Spaniard. Filipino fighters always removed the Mauser's rear sight. They thought sighting through its pinhole took too much time. The front sight was enough for them."

He took the Mauser and aimed it at a target, an empty bottle. He fired. *Bung-bung!* The bottle was still there.

"Naturally, the missing rear sight made them aim too high."

He fired again. A hit this time.

"Let me try the Remington," José Ma. Basa said.

"The gun that killed Rizal," said Padre Guinbaolibot.

"Yes, I know," said José Ma. Basa. He fired at a row of bottles. *Pac-bung!* A hit.

"Very different sound," said Dr. Lugay. "During the war, everyone could tell whether a gun was a Remington or a Mauser just by its sound."

José Ma. Basa fired again. Another hit. And another. Three hits in all.

"Very good," said the widow. "As easy as assassinating the Bonifacio brothers."

"You know," Dr. Lugay said, "Kapitan Miong wouldn't have done it. Then one of the Magdiwang generals told him Bonifacio was planning to liquidate *him*."

"So he decided to pre-empt Bonifacio," she said.

"It's all history now," José Ma. Basa said. "Where's Aguinaldo today? Probably rusticating on his farm in Cavíte. He's got some 200 hectares in Lumil. That's in Silang, Cavíte."

"The Americans duped him not once, but thrice," Dr. Lugay said.

"Consuls Wildman and Pratt," José Ma. Basa said. "Who's the third?"

"Colonel Funston, the one who captured him. Naturally, they promoted him for that. He's now Brigadier General Funston."

"Why do you say he duped Aguinaldo?" asked Doña Trining.

"It may have been the only way to capture him. Of course, it wasn't quite cricket, as the English would say."

"Oh, but all is fair," said José Ma. Basa, "in love and war."

"True, true. When Funston broke Aguinaldo's code and sent him false messages in it, via the traitor Major Hilario Talplacido, that was fair enough. When he took Macabebe scouts who pretended they were Tagalogs, that was fair enough. If the ostensible leader was that double turncoat Lázaro Segovia, it was highly appropriate. Segovia was a Spaniard who defected to the winning side twice, first to the Filipinos and then to the Americans. When Funston let it appear he was their prisoner and they were delivering him to Aguinaldo, that was fair enough. When his force ran out of food a few miles from Aguinaldo's hideout in Palanan and he sent some of the Macabebes to beg for food from his enemy, it was within his rights to do so. But after he had eaten of that food, any action against the enemy had become taboo."

"I see what you mean," said Padre Guinbaolibot. "That food, coming as it did from the enemy, was sacred. Once Funston had eaten of it, Aguinaldo should have become inviolate, at least for that time."

"I didn't know he stooped so low," said José Ma. Basa. "Saul would not let his men eat before doing battle with the Philistines, not even wild honey off the trees."

"More than that," said the priest, "when you eat food in a strange place it binds you in some mysterious way to that place, and to whoever gave you that food. That is why the Greek goddess Ceres was cautioned not to eat anything when she was in Hades visiting her dead husband. In like manner, we are changed by the bread we eat at the Eucharist."

"In short," said Dr. Lugay, "Funston committed sacrilege."

"What about General Antonio Luna's assassination?" asked Doña Trining. "Didn't your Kapitan Miong have something to do with that, too?"

"I wouldn't know, *señora*," Dr. Lugay said.

Months later, in 1908, José Ma. Basa wangled a return to Manila, accepting the post of bookkeeper at the Estrella del Norte shipping line. A year and a half passed before a First Mate's position became vacant and he was called upon to fill it. Finally he was going back to sea. It was his true calling. From here on, no more postings in the judiciary. No more awkward questions about the Brigandage Act, or the Flag Law that made it a crime to display national flags that were not of stars and stripes. No looking back. He would remain a mariner until he was a pillar, encrusted with salt, of the maritime community.

He sailed all around the archipelago in the years from 1909 through 1913, with the sporadic haul to far-flung ports: Piraeus, Ajaccio, Southampton once; Lae, Suva, Sydney another time. He was away from home a good deal, but not too much. He had a loving wife, adorable children, and the sea for a mistress.

Bad news came from Guiuan in 1911: Ninay had suffered a stroke. They rushed over, he and Chichang, leaving the children in Manila. The stroke had rendered Ninay a paralytic from the waist down. She was 33. The rest of her life would have to be in a wheelchair.

The tragedy of the *Titanic* sinking on her maiden voyage in 1912 shocked him. He could not understand it. How could her crew be so careless? He had kept many a night watch at sea, and never begrudged the loss of sleep it cost him.

In 1914 he gained his first command, the good ship *San Nicolas*. He took naturally to being Captain Basa. At sea he could now delegate many of the routine tasks to his Chief Mate and crew. Now he could write poetry and paint a little. He had always been a scribbler and a doodler, at idle moments, even as a schoolboy. A lone seagull once followed the *San Nicolas* for hours on end. Finally he wrote a poem about it, "A Una Gaviota":

> *Tengo envidia de ti, blanca gaviota,*
> *porque puedes vola cuando tu quieras*

Simple enough, no fancy lines. It was nothing compared to Coleridge's "Rime of the Ancient Mariner" but this was not an albatross. He finished that quatrain, then wrote another:

> *Tengo envidia de ti, porque es mi anhelo*
> *poder tambien volar. Yo necesito,*
> *para alejarme de este inmundo suelo,*
> *con mis alas subin al infinito.*

And so the seagull's wings had become a metaphor for his longing. He wrote three more stanzas, pursuing thoughts he was not sure he could pin down.

> *Feliz al que, cual tu, puede alejarse*
> *de este asfixiante mundo y de su ruido,*
> *y en el eter purisimo inebriarse,*
> *o en alta roca fabricar su nido.*

Just so. Ether was breathed not drank, and it left one anesthetized not drunk, but it rhymed. One more stanza to wrap it up, and it was done.

Being at sea was good for poetry. The sea was good for the soul. Sea and soul both were irregular words, *mar* being both masculine and feminine, while *alma* was masculine. Soon he had written another poem, "El Mar y El Alma":

> *Y brisa susurrante que vuela ensuaves giros,*
> *Llevando entre sus alas murmurios de la mar;*
> *lo mismo tiene alma sus vuelos y suspiros,*
> *que cual sutil incienso van a su dulce hogar...*

Seven stanzas in all, of which that quatrain eventually became the middle. The poem was later published in the *Boletin Marítimo*.

His career was going well. World War I came to an end, a distant conflict on the other side of the world. In 1918 he was appointed to the *S.S. Neil Macleod*, a bigger, better and faster ship. He liked the poetry of the Spaniard, Gustavo Adolfo Becquer, so much that he wrote a poem in the latter's style. Naturally, he called it "Becquerianas." Its final stanza went

> *Y en mi alma horriblemente lacerada,*
> *ay quien sabe si no se borraran,*
>
> *las huellas que mis ultimos llores*
> *dejaron al pasar!*

In 1921 he was reassigned again, this time to the *M.V. Albay*. His firstborn son, Antonio, following in his footsteps, was at nautical school. Toñing's grades were topnotch, and won the boy a year's stint at the US Naval Academy in Annapolis, Maryland. The young man returned to become a Second Mate on the *M.V. Batangas* the following year.

His eldest son was already a *marinero* while his youngest daughter, Herminia, was still an infant. He did not know it yet, but he and Chichang were to have two more, Francisco and Remedios.

Any Filipino poet who wrote in Spanish sooner or later found an opportunity to sing to Rizal. It was understood that one had to employ a style similar to those of Rizal's best poems. There could be no holding back; one had to declaim in the grand manner. He toiled over " A Rizal," all four stanzas of it, for a long time:

*Bajo del plomo faral de aquel sicario*
*Sucumbiste es verdad, mas no tu idea*
*que, cual luz increada centella*
*desde el fondo del ambito estelario.*

*Con un valor heroico y temerario,*
*cual un nuevo Hombre-Dios de otra Judea,*
*diste tu vida a que tu Patria vea*
*que no hay rendencion sin un calvario!*

*Si sales de esa tumba en que reposas*
*y vieras las tragedias dolorosas*
*que en nuestra Patria se han desarrollado;*

*Y hallar no logres ya hombre viriles,*
*sino hipócritas, parías y serviles...*
*volveras a tu tumba horrorizado!*

He was aware that the poem bore some resemblance to Cecilio Apostol's own "A Rizal," published in Luna's *La Independencia* in 1898 under the pen name "Catulo." He could not remember how that poem went, except for random lines like *"latter-day messiah of a land in bondage"* or *"sleep in peace in the shadows of nothing."* Apostol had ended the poem with something like *"though a bullet shat-*

*tered the white walls of your skull/ Your ideas destroyed the ramparts of an empire.*" In the Basa version the order had been inverted and the poem made to begin with the bullet. Perhaps this was an improvement. The thought was immodest, but he kept it to himself.

Now the years were going faster. Toñing, his eldest son, was following his footsteps in another way: the boy was planning to get married young. His hermano político's three eldest children, Peping, Licoy and Soling, had come from Guiuan to attend university in Manila. Now Toñing, a First Mate on the *M.V. Samar*, had fallen in love with Soling. It was a bit of a scandal, with a whiff of incest about it, but the lovers were headstrong and would have it no other way. Within the prohibited degrees of consanguinity a Papal dispensation was required, not only to permit this marriage of first cousins but also to legitimize its issue. When it was learned that the family indeed intended to apply for one, through the office of Archbishop O'Doherty of Manila, Carolina and Licoy revealed their own love for each other. This was too much! Two pairs of cousins wanting to marry! There was nothing to be done but apply for another dispensation.

His youngest daughter, Remedios, was born in 1924, and so was Dr. Lugay's, Nieves. Remedios was Chichang's 22nd pregnancy but only the eleventh to survive. Nieves was Dr. Lugay's daughter by some local woman. A dozen years after his wife became an invalid, the good doctor had finally committed an indiscretion.

The first dispensation duly arrived from Rome, and Antonio Basa married Soledad Lugay late in 1924. The Lugay family, Ninay in her wheelchair, came to Manila from Guiuan for the wedding. José Ma. Basa and Dr. José

Lugay now found themselves *compadres*. Ninay and Chichang were now sisters and *comadres* at the same time. Chichang carried her newest baby, Remedios, born earlier that year, in her arms. Whenever the baby was asleep she would lay it on Ninay's lap in the wheelchair.

The second dispensation arrived, and it sanctioned the union of Carolina Basa and Rafael Lugay in 1925. That same year José M. Basa, as he wrote his name now, was reassigned yet again, and became the captain of the *M.V. Luzon*. In 1926 he became a grandfather with the birth of Toñing's first child, Angel. Dr. Lugay became a grandfather simultaneously, and of the same boy. They had a grandson in common now.

Only the resonance of the phrase remained, but now he wanted to write a poem under the title "Fatal Augurio." All he had were a few vague ideas, but he would make the effort.

He picked up his pen. The muse must have filled it with magic ink, for the poem practically wrote itself:

> *No es que yo vea el mundo tan sombrio*
> *ni me dómina un hondo pesimismo;*
> *pero mi corazon de fe vacío*
> *excluye de mi mente el optisimo.*

There was more, but the pen had dried up. Another time, perhaps. Strange, how he could begin it so easily and yet be unable to write further. In his mind he saw the poem as a series of quatrains, but he had no idea how many quatrains there might be. Most of his poems, if written in quatrains, had six or nine; his minimum was four, like "A Rizal" or "Envio." The longest he had done had fourteen, "En Mi Soledad." The seventh quatrain of that went

> *Trabaja, juventud, si tu deseas*
> *Ver la semilla florecer un día;*
> *No importa que en el campo luego veas*
> *El espectro del hambre y la agonía...*

Quatrains had written themselves for that poem, but now the knack had deserted him. How did one finish a poem with a title like "Fatal Augurio"?

Toñing's second child was born in 1927, a daughter. His first granddaughter. Over his objections she was named after him: Josefina Basa. Now his homonyms included one on the distaff side. "Neníta," he cooed when the infant curled her hand around his finger. The nickname, spontaneously bestowed, stuck.

Poetry failed him in 1929. His world caved in: Chichang died very suddenly of a heart attack. She was too young to die, only 44, and it was cruel for her to be taken away when their youngest daughter was only 5 and their youngest son 7. It was totally unfair.

José M. Basa spent the next few weeks in a daze, not understanding how he got through the wake, the funeral, the nine days of prayer...

He never wrote a poem about his loss. The grief was too great for words. But once, his daughters said, he gave way to it and shouted to the sky: "*Nada y nada y nada!*"

Questing for something that might heal his soul, he reported back for duty. His dark moods made him wangle an assignment that would again take him around the world. In twenty years of sailing his farthest west had been Bristol and Glasgow; he had sailed east to Vancouver and San Francisco, then gone through the Panama Canal and steamed north to New York and later up the St. Lawrence River to Montreal. But he had yet to cross the Atlantic and complete a clean circumnavigation.

Manila to Batavia, where he exchanged the cargo of copra and abaca for a load of tin and rubber, was routine sailing. His true self was somewhere else; it was another part of him that crossed the Indian Ocean to Bombay, then Aden. He functioned as an automaton, guiding his ship through the Red Sea while he himself stood apart. He felt uninvolved as they went through the Suez Canal and made stops at Port Said, Valletta, and Genoa. He left the handling of the cargo and the purchase of provisions to his able subordinates. His forte was navigation, but his sextant found the current latitude all by itself. He stood his share of the night watches, but when he took star sightings the cold light of those distant suns seemed to be mocking him.

From Genoa it was a few days to Barcelona, where another captain from his shipping line was waiting. The relief captain would take the ship back to Manila. Captain Basa was to proceed on his own to Cherbourg, where he would assume command of another of the line's vessels, which was due there in a month.

Barcelona at the height of summer seemed a city meant for a younger man. He saw Montjuich, lit a candle for Chichang at the Catedrál de La Sagrada Família. The cathedral was his junior by a year. Construction had begun in 1882 and now, in 1929, it was far from finished. From Catalonia he took the coastal road down Valencia and Murcia as far as the town of Lorca, then turned inland to the small town of Baza in the hilly eastern backwoods of Andalusia. Baza must have been the origin of his name; perhaps he had distant relatives there. He stayed overnight, drinking brandy, then left for Granada. After stopping to see the Alhambra, he went to the Mezquita. Inside the beautiful Moorish mosque was a baroque cathedral. It was an intrusion, and he cursed the religious intolerants who had built it. They should have left the mosque alone.

In Sevilla he knelt down to pray inside Europe's largest Gothic cathedral. He admired the tomb of Columbus, the cathedral's five aisles, and the paintings by Zurbarán and Murillo. He wondered about the mortal remains of Christopher Columbus. Were the bones here more authentic than those in Hispaniola? His thoughts went to Gen. Trujillo. If the man could win his revolution, there would soon be a Dominican Republic.

He found the Iglesia Parroquial de Paradas and there viewed El Greco's painting, "Santa María Magdalena." He remembered the model had supposedly been Doña Jerónima de las Cuevas, who had borne El Greco a son but would not give her hand to him in marriage.

He went to the bullfights, then to the tapas bars for *gazpacho, calamares en su tinta, jamón jabugo, mazapan*. He stayed up until four in the morning, as the natives did, drinking sherry and nibbling tapas.

He was eating five meals a day in the Spanish manner, starting with a *desayuno* of *churros con chocolate* upon rising at 9 a.m. Then the *almuerzo* at 11, a meal known in English only by the American barbarism "brunch." The *comida* would be served at 2:30, a heavy meal with soup or salad, baked fish with red cabbage and a dry white wine, or *cocido* and red wine, *leche flan* or fruit, coffee and brandy. He would have a *merienda* of coffee and pastries at 6 p.m., and the *cena* only after sunset. Because it was summer, the sun never set before 10 p.m. If he had made the usual round of the tapas bars, he would do as the natives did and dine between midnight and 2:00 a.m.

Routine greetings, too, had to be adjusted. In Manila one began with "buenos días" in the morning and changed to "buenos tardes" promptly at the stroke of noon, moving on to "buenas noches" immediately after praying the Angelus at 6:00 p.m. In Spain the clock had less influence over these things than the fact of having ingested one's meals. One continued to use "buenos días" until he had eaten his *comida*. It was correct to say "buenos tardes" from then on until one sat down to the *cena*. Often it was well nigh midnight before he greeted anyone with "buenas noches."

In Toledo he wanted only to see more paintings by El Greco. Domenicos Theotokopoulus, yes, that was the man's name, a painter from Crete who had apprenticed under Titian.

In the Iglesia de Santo Tomé he marveled at the "Entierro del Conde de Orgaz," depicting an event that had happened in 1323. According to legend, St. Stephen and St. Augustine had both come down from Heaven to bury the late Count of Orgaz, Don Gonzálo Ruíz de Toledo. The dead Count, in full armor minus the helmet, looked like someone he knew. He couldn't remember who. All of the men attending the burial were bearded and mustachioed, but one man was clean-shaven, and this man reminded him somewhat of his uncle and namesake, José María Basa. St. Augustine looked like the old parish priest of the town of Baza, if one could mentally substitute a simple *soutane* for the bishop's ornate gold-brocaded vestments. One of the Covarrubias brothers looked like a man he had passed on the street a few moments before. One of the Knights of Santiago resembled a daguerreotype of his uncle Matías Basa as a young man. Another Knight of Santiago, he knew, had been modeled on Cervantes. El Greco had included his son Jorge Manuel, too, as the pageboy in the foreground. El Greco himself was the man standing behind St. Augustine, looking like a distinguished man José M. Basa had seen in Sevilla...a retired matador.

In the Toledo Cathedral he viewed the "Espolio," Jesus Christ about to be disrobed before being nailed to the cross, the Roman centurions around Him in medieval Spanish armor. The Three Marys were also present, another of El Greco's "theological errors." In the Cathedral's Sacristia Mayor he looked at the "Martirio de San Mauricio." He remembered the verse from the Gospel of Matthew that was supposed to apply to this painting, "Be ye therefore wise as serpents, and sinless as doves."

In a shop near the Cathedral he ordered a sword, of the kind a conquistador might have worn. He had always wanted a weapon of Toledo steel. The proprietor asked if he wanted the blade's final quenching to be in oil or in water, or both. He chose water.

The Toledo sky was overcast, lending it a gloomy aspect. This was the mood in El Greco's "View of Toledo," not the one with the street map but the famous one, of the city transfigured. He wished the original were not in New York. The painting's whereabouts had been unknown for years, but only a few months before he had read a curious item in the papers. A Mrs. H. O. Havemeyer had died, around the same time Chichang had died, and in her will bequeathed the "View of Toledo" to the Metropolitan Museum of Art. There was no justice in the art world. By all rights that painting should never have left Toledo.

He left the Cathedral and walked all the way to the old city wall. He crossed the Rio Tajo on the Puente Alcántara.

On the opposite bank, he turned right and walked on until he reached El Greco's vantage point. The spire of the Cathedral just so; the turrets of the Alcázar just so. The bend in the river, too. He had to walk much farther than he might have thought. He saw at once that El Greco had altered the topography to heighten certain effects in the painting. He stood there gazing, the wind clutching at his hair, marveling at how well the Greek had exercised artistic license. He wondered how the artist would have painted the city had he come to it in an earlier era, during Toledo's most glorious period, the time of the Moors. But perhaps the poignant mood El Greco captured was that of a city that could only sigh for its lost glories. He sighed himself, remembering his own losses, his solitude, his anomies. A light rain began to fall.

In Madrid he had only a few hours to tour the Prado. He went straight to the paintings of Goya and Velásquez. Then it was time to go to Paris.

He flew in an aëroplane for the first time, Madrid-Paris in a Fokker tri-motor, landing at Le Bourget. He hoped the pilot would circle the Eiffel Tower, as Lindbergh had done two years before, but no such thing happened.

In Paris he rushed through the Louvre, knowing he had to come again some other time. Da Vinci's "Mona Lisa" was there, and so were works by the French Impressionists...and by Spaniards like Picasso and Miró. He found transportation to Le Havre despite his execrable French. At a village along the way there was some confusion about numbers when he paid for a meal. He thought the *"quatre-vingts"* he was being charged meant 4 francs 20 centimes. After the proprietor protested he realized it meant 80 francs. He had forgotten his grammar school French. One could count by tens only up to 60 (*seisenta*, *soixante*). It was different when one came to 70 (*setenta*) or 80 (*ochenta*). There were no such words as "septante" or "huitante." Instead, one had to say *soixante-dix* or "sixty-ten" and *quatre-vingts* or "four twenties." Of course 90 (*noventa*) was not "neufante" but *quatre-vingts-dix*. All a remnant of some old Celtic way of counting. Atavistic, but what could one expect of the Gauls?

In Le Havre he managed to get on a small boat that was going to Cherbourg.

He assumed command of the *M. V. Luzon*. She was ready to sail. He set out across the Bay of Biscay and then south to Lisbon.

The crossing of the Atlantic was routine. A stop at Funchal in the Madeiras, where they took on as many barrels of the island's superb wine as they could, then on to Brazil.

Running with the trades, the weeks blurred into one another. He tasted the Madeira. It was sweet but good. The barrels were big, big enough for drowning in. He knew an English duke had drowned in just such a barrel. Or had it been an earl?

He was in Recife a few days, then Rio de Janeiro. In both places the Brazilians refused to talk in Spanish, preferring French, which always piqued him, or English. He was glad to reach Buenos Aires, where it seemed everyone he met spoke Spanish like a Madrileño, had an Italian name, and thought himself an Englishman.

Scheduled to go north and cross the Panama Canal, his orders were changed. Now he was to go through the Strait of Magellan.

Steaming south, he found the magnetic compass variation in those waters to be unusually large. It was his first encounter with the so-called South Atlantic Anomaly.

His last Atlantic port of call was Puerto Deseado. He slowed down going past Puerto San Julian, which he scanned with his binoculars. He imagined the gibbets still stood there, the ones from which Magellan hanged Mendoza and Quesada, and from which Drake hanged Thomas Doughty.

The Strait of Magellan proved devilishly difficult. A strong wind was always blowing, usually in a direction contrary to the current. He kept all hands on alert for the dreaded williwaw, the wind that came without warning from nowhere, usually with enough force to capsize a square-rigger. His ship did not have sails, but if she caught a williwaw at a bad angle she could also be damaged. He remembered that García de Loaysa's ships had been dragged ashore, in 1526, by a williwaw in the Bahia Posesión just past the entrance to the Strait.

The current kept changing, depending on whether it was ebb or flood tide from the Atlantic or, further on, from the Pacific. He stopped briefly at Punta Arenas half-way through the Strait. He wondered if he would ever pass that way again. Cold and desolate and beautiful, the place haunted something in his soul. Snowcapped mountains drew one's gaze down to waterfalls emptying directly into the sea. The Strait was much longer than he had always supposed. He marked it off on the chart with a pair of dividers and found it to be some 334 nautical miles, from Punta Dungeness at the Atlantic entrance to the rocky shoals called the Evangelistas at the Pacific exit. That was about the distance by sea from Manila to Cebú.

Debouching into the Pacific, he sailed north until he found the Humboldt Current, then turned northwest. The compass variation there was still very great, some 14 or 15 degrees east from true North. He made detailed entries in his logbook. "In an area of east variation," he could still hear Lt. Cooper's voice from his Nautical Academy days, "the compass is always the smaller figure when converting." It was fatally easy to apply the correction the wrong way, but Cooper had a mnemonic for it: "Variation west, compass reads best; variation east, compass reads least."

He recalled another of Cooper's mnemonics: "Starboard light is green, port light is red." Some of his classmates could never remember which was which, until Cooper told them to say "port wine is red." That was how they always said it now: "Starboard light is green, port wine is red."

Someday he would write a textbook for mariners. His years of sailing experience would go into it, and so would all his mnemonics.

His first sight of land in the Pacific was Pukapuka in the Tuamoto Archipelago, latitude given as 14°38' South, longitude 138°19' West. His French charts from the *Hydrographique de la Marine* gave the sounding near Pukapuka as 2010 metres, over a thousand fathoms. He felt sure it was the island Magellan had called the Isla de San Pablo. Probably the same island sighted by le Maire and Schouten in 1616. Because Magellan's sounding leads extended for only 200 fathoms, the pioneer had considered those depths bottomless. Desperate for food and fresh water, Magellan had been unable to anchor and stop at San Pablo.

He passed Caroline Islet, one of the Line Islands of French Polynesia, although it was now under British sovereignty, and not to be confused with the Caroline Islands of Micronesia much farther west. Caroline had to be the second island passed in the Pacific by Magellan, who had called it the Isla de Tiburónes. He calculated its position to be at latitude 10°02' South, longitude 150°43' West. It was an atoll with a lagoon full of fish. The fish would draw hordes of sharks, hence Magellan's name for the island. Caroline formed a triangle with two other islets, Flint some 125 miles to the southwest, and Vostok about the same distance to the west. Both were rocky pinnacles rising from the sea, full of seabirds and, presumably, guano. Both islets had also been proposed as *the* Isla de Tiburónes, although he could see now that only Caroline had a lagoon to attract sharks. The charts gave the sounding as 1370 metres, about 770 fathoms. Magellan had also been unable to attain that island. It must have been quite a frustrating experience.

His first stop in the Pacific was Guam, as Magellan's had been. He hove to in Umatac, on the island's lee side. He remembered that his uncle José María Basa, together with Antonio María Regidor and Balbino Mauricio, had escaped from that island in 1874.

He entered the Philippine archipelago through the narrow San Bernardino Strait, more of a challenge than the Surigao Strait. He threaded his way among the familiar islands for a couple of days, and finally steamed into Manila Bay. A harbor pilot came aboard to guide his ship in. Somehow, as the captain, he secretly resented it. He had no need of a pilot to bring his ship into his home port.

As he ordered Finished With Engines, the captain's last command on every voyage, he wished he had cannon on board, so he could fire a broadside in salute.

South to the Visayas in 1930, when he was appointed Port Captain of Cebú. (In those days it was always spelled with the accent.) He moved to that city with his four youngest children, Rosario, Herminia, Francisco, and Remedios, living on shipboard until he found a house on Jones Avenue. His eldest, Toñing, a Chief Mate on the *M. V. Mindanao*, soon followed, moving into a house on Calle Sanciangco. Toñing had three children now, Angel, Josefina and Antonio Jr.; Toñing's wife Soling was pregnant with their fourth. José M. Basa's second eldest, Carolina, lived in Guiuan with her husband, Licoy Lugay, and their sons, Fernando and José (another namesake!) while Arturo and Ernesto, both newly married, remained in Manila. With them lived their sisters Carmen, Narcisa, Soledad, and Rosario, all attending schools in Manila.

His house was not far from Sergio Osmeña's on the same street. The Senator lived in Manila, in the house his second wife's parents had given them, but came to Cebú as often as possible, usually on weekends.

He first met Don Sergio socially at a dinner given by a woman named Pilar Herrera. This lady had attended the

University of Santo Tomás in Manila, where one of her classmates had been Esperanza Limjap, now married to Senator Osmeña.

"A pleasure to make your acquaintance, Capitán Basa. How are you related to the Cavíte mutineer...the one who lived in Hongkong?"

"My uncle."

"Well now, I hear you have only recently lost your wife. I commiserate with you."

Don Sergio could speak with some authority on the subject. He had married his first wife, Estefania Chiong-Veloso, in 1901, the same year José M. Basa married Chichang. Don Sergio and Doña Pepang had thirteen children, of whom ten survived infancy. While delivering the thirteenth in 1918, Doña Pepang had died in childbirth. Mother and child had both been lost. Don Sergio married again in 1920. His second wife, Titay Limjap of Manila, had borne him three more children.

"Allow me to give you a word of advice, young man," Don Sergio told him. "You must marry again."

He took Don Sergio's word seriously and kept his eyes open for a suitable woman. There was no shortage of them in Cebú. There was Pilar Herrera of course, a well-educated, refined lady who spoke Spanish, French, English, Visayan, and Tagalog, as well as the Chinese dialects spoken in Cebú and Shanghai; a classic *chinita* beauty. But he had always preferred the Filipina or Spanish types.

He began courting a woman named Felicissima Najarro. She was thirtyish and very pretty, especially when she wore a mantilla, which set off her Spanish mestiza features. The whole thing must have gone badly, for the only trace left of it was the poem he wrote, entitled "Adios," dedicated to "feli-Naj." It was highly emotional, not typical of him, not in his usual style:

> *Mujer sin corazon!...Mujer sin alma!...*
> *Sigue tu senda de fragrantes flores,*
> *Mientras recorro con fingida calma,*
> *El camino sin luz, mis dolores.*

And then there was the woman called Aurora, another mestiza. Very young, about half his age...

A poem he wrote, "A Una Bayadera," summed it all up; the title translated as "To One Who Doesn't Care":

> *Te ame con ciego amor al verte, Aurora,*
> *porque en tu faz de sierpe tentadora*
> *crei advertir las huellas de tu encanto;*
> *y te halle abandonada a tu destino*
> *en un aspero y tetrico camino*
> *donde has espinas y dolor y llanto...*

He had shown this poem to her. As with many in her generation she was more comfortable with English than Spanish, and so callow as to coo over how well he could write and how she was going to try and translate it. What exquisite torture! He sat through it, squirming as he watched her treat his poem as a mere exercise in translation.

> *On seeing you I loved you with a blind love, Aurora*

*Because on your serpent-tempting face*
*I believed you cried out traces*
*of your charm and I found*
*abandoned on a rough and melancholy road*
*your destiny of thorns, pain, and tears...*

Her translation was passable, except for the second line: "serpent-tempting face" sounded strange. Perhaps it was literally correct but "face that tempts like the serpent" would have been more exact. But, clearly, neither form had the force of the Spanish original, nor the allusion to Eve's baser qualities that Adam and most men after him usually succumbed to. It did not matter, of course. She had missed the message entirely.

There was never enough time for the things that mattered. He wasted too much time on poetry, and on painting, too. In Montreal, the farthest north he had been, he had once seen the aurora borealis. Something in the eerie beauty of that natural phenomenon now became mixed up, in his mind, with strange memories of the woman named Aurora. He began an oil painting of it, as impressionistic as anything the French *pinteurs* were doing, but nothing more than a graphic representation, with faithful colors, of the northern lights.

He managed another stanza for "Fatal Augurio."

*Y llego al estudiar con juicio frio,*
*nuestro aparente o falso patriotismo*
*llena de espanto el pensamiento mio*

*la idea de un futuro cataclismo.*


He let it languish there, with its fearful ideas. Other matters were more immediate, and more deserving of his attention. The ritual of Sunday dinner, for example. Every Sunday Toñing, Soling and their three children would come over for the noontime meal. He had a large dining table, and enjoyed sitting at its head with his children and grandchildren around him. Carolina, Licoy, and their two sons came over every other Sunday; they now lived in Bogó, a town at the northern tip of Cebú, where Licoy ran a pharmacy, the Farmacia Lugay.

Lunch was the *comida*. Usually his eldest son's family came early enough for the *almuerzo*, too. His daughter-in-law was mistress of the kitchen every Sunday, as Soling was much the best cook in the whole family. Although she had grown up in Guiuan, she had learned her cooking from her mother, an eloquent exponent of Caviteño cuisine.

Soling combined disparate dishes in ways only Caviteños ever did. She would serve an *escabeche* of whatever fish was at hand, usually *banak* or *tangguingue*, with *mongo guisado*. In Cebú tangguingue was called tangigî; the difference seemed to bespeak a want of refinement, but it was the same fish.

Soling always served *lechon kawali* with chicken *pochero*. Beef *pochero*, on the other hand, was best eaten with fried *lumpia* or a *torta* of ground pork. An *embutido* revealed its subtle flavors only when eaten with *kamias na buro*, a sour fruit called *ibà* in Cebú; an *estofado* lacked depth without fried *hasa-hasa*; and *lechon paksiw* was colorless without its complement, *tuyo*. They could not find *tuyo* in Cebú;

they always had to make do with Visayan versions of dried
fish.

Under steam again, sailing the high seas. In 1932 Pilar
Herrera was a passenger on a Manila-Shanghai run.
When it was her turn to grace the captain's table he inter-
viewed her. Her father, Uy Chi Hon, had left Canton as a
young man in 1870 and settled in Cebú, converting to
Christianity and assuming his baptismal sponsor's surname
to become Lucio Herrera. He married a Cebuana, Fe Llamas. His brother-in-law, Francisco Llamas, organized a
revolutionary movement and Lucio Herrera became its
Treasurer. The movement's revolt of April 3, 1898 was
quelled in a few days, but turned that day, Tres de Abril,
into a rallying cr· for succeeding revolts. In 1905 Lucio
Herrera, who had not surrendered his Chinese nationality,
had been appointed Chinese consul in Cebú, a post he
held until his death in 1925.

Pilar had spent her growing years in Cebú and Shanghai. Then she had gone to Manila to study at the University of Santo Tomás, and after that to Paris for two years
at the Sorbonne. Now she would be spending several
months in Shanghai. Next year she would be revisiting
Paris...

She knew the way to Shanghai better than he did. Turn
west into the Yangtze River, sail upstream with eyes peeled
for the spot where the Huangpu River emptied into the
Yangtze. From the Yangtze turn south into the much nar-
rower Huangpu, and follow its gentle curves until one
caught sight of the Bund.

She stayed at the Peace Hotel, and invited him to dinner there. His schedule was tight, but he found the time.

There seemed to be more Europeans than Chinese in that part of Shanghai, and the two of them felt no incongruity in dining on French cuisine. She asked if he would be in Paris in the next few months or so. He said it was probable, but he would have to check his schedule at the home office in Manila. Then, before the dancing began, he had to go.

On the return voyage to Manila he wrote another stanza for "Fatal Augurio":

> *Ya lo veremos con dolor la ruina,*
>
> *de esta bendita raza filipina;*
>
> *y de su misma religion la muerte;*

He left it there, hanging by a semicolon.

Vast and timeless, the Pacific seemed to seethe with hidden forces. It matched his own moods, feelings kept just under the surface. The year was 1933, but it could have been 1520, for all the Pacific Ocean cared, or 1000 AD.

Manila-Yokohama was a routine leg. From Japan he sailed east at 40°N, on the track Padre Andrés de Urdaneta had pioneered. Cape Mendocino was his landfall, and he made a stop in San Francisco. At sea again, he turned south, went through the Panama Canal, then put in at Havana. From there, New York.

He thought of wresting the Blue Ribband of the Atlantic from the *Normandie* or the *Queen Elizabeth*, whichever of them currently held it, but it was an idle musing. On his next leg, New York-Cherbourg, the ship was full of Americans, the women dressed as flappers and dancing

the Charleston or the foxtrot to such silly tunes as "Would
You Rather be a Colonel with an Eagle on your Shoulder
or a Private With a Chicken on Your Knee?" and even the
truly ghastly "Is You or Isn't You Ain't Not My Baby?"
Those *gringos*! So frivolous. So eager to get away from
their homeland and Prohibition, and on to a ship where
the liquor flowed freely.

In Paris he went to the Louvre, intending as full a tour
as he could manage.

He could not appreciate the paintings. His mind was
not on art.

He crossed the Seine at the Pont des Arts and, in the
Left Bank, began looking for the Place St-Sulpice. It was
not hard to find; the St-Sulpice church dominated the park.
He walked around the park until he found the Rue des
Canettes, and the Hôtel Récamier. At the front desk, he
asked if Pilar Herrera had checked in.

Indeed she had, said the concierge. Was *monsieur* expected? No, but he would be most grateful if *madame* could be
informed of his presence...

Pilar did not care for museums. They walked around
the Left Bank, strolling aimlessly. La Rive Gauche, she
called it. He refused to speak French. Her command of
the language was good, and she had the accent and savoir-
faire of the Parisienne. When they had to speak to the
natives, he let her do the talking.

They found a café, took a sidewalk table, and had coffee and croissants. The Eiffel Tower was visible in the
distance. Night fell, and they saw that thousands of light
bulbs on the Eiffel Tower had been arranged to spell out
CITROËN vertically, in seven colors. The spelling, as Pilar

pointed out, was meticulously correct: there were two dots over the E.


They walked the streets. They drank pastis in Les Deux Magots on St-Germain des Prés. They had dinner at La Coupole on Boulevard du Montparnasse, where arriving patrons had to pass through a maze of benches and tables as if on exhibit. Everyone could see everyone arriving, and that was why the restaurant was so popular: everyone went there to be seen. Traditionally, artists and bohemian types sat on the left, the bourgeoisie on the right. He was going to take a table on the right, but Pilar steered him to one on the left.

"You write poetry, don't you? That makes you an artist."

"I'm no bohemian. Everything rhymes."

"No matter. We must sit on the left. I feel more like a bohemian than a bourgeois tonight."

While waiting for their *cassoulet* and *choucroute garnie* they watched more customers arrive. A man came in leading a lobster on a leash. "He's an artist," they overheard a woman at the next table tell her companion. "Dadaist, so they say."

They went to a show, he could not remember where, which featured the singing of Edith Piaf. Later they found themselves at the Notre Dame, admiring it by moonlight. From there they strolled to the tip of the Île de la Cité, to the Square du Vert-Galant. Couples could be seen kissing.

*"Increíble,"* he said.

"You seem to find that shocking," Pilar said.

"Not at all," he said. "I was just thinking, when in Rome, do as the Romans do."

Slowly he took her in his arms, began to do as the French did.

They were married on September 29, 1933, in the Basilica Minore del Santo Niño de Cebú. He was 52, but did not look it. His family was blessed with a rare genetic trait: their hair remained black well into old age; an aunt of his had died at 88 or 89 with a full head of jet-black hair. He was much younger than that, and he had no gray in his hair at all. Pilar was still a youth at 38, only seven years older than his firstborn son. As she started up the aisle he almost choked for seeing how beautiful she really was, and what a close thing it had been. The others had almost made a fool out of him. He had come to his senses in time; now he understood that his fate lay with Pilar. He was a very fortunate man.

She was being given away by her uncle, Francisco Llamas, the leader of the 1898 Tres de Abril revolt.

His hermano político, Dr. José Lugay, stood beside him as his best man. Senator and Mrs. Osmeña knelt as sponsors. His eldest granddaughter, six-year-old Neníta, was a flower girl. Neníta's brother, four-year-old Antonio Jr., was the ringbearer.

He was as nervous as he had been during his first wedding, when he was 20. He fumbled when it was time to take the rings from the pillow his four-year-old grandson Antonio Jr. carried, nearly dropping the rings on the floor. Later, when they turned around to face the congregation, he almost tripped on Pilar's wedding gown train...

He had written a poem for Pilar, "Lo que yo quiero." At the reception, after they had cut the wedding cake, he surprised her with it. He recited his new poem from memory, with appropriate gestures, to tumultuous applause:

*Quisiera ser la brisa que vaga entre las flores,*
*para darte el aroma y el mas suave frescor;*
*quisiera ser al ave que vuela en los alcores,*
*para arrullar tu sueño con canticos de amor.*
*Quisiera ser el blando finisimo pañuelo,*
*en donde a veces sueles tus lagrimas verter,*
*para sacar tus ojos, hermosos como el cielo,*
*y el llanto que tu viertes poderlo recojer.*

*Quisiera ser la imagen del santo escapulario,*
*que llevas en tu pecho constanta devoción,*
*para sentir el grato calor de este santuario,*
*en que feliz palpita tu tierno corazon.*

*Quisiera ser el agua de fuente cristalina—*
*que en la espesura umbria sepea a su merced—*
*que codiciosa bebas en anfora ambarina*
*para besar tus labios, para calmar tu sed.*

*Quisiera ser, bien mio, tu idolatrada sombra,*
*para poder seguirte por donde quier que vas;*
*Porque en mis tristes horas mi corazon te nombra*
*y mi alma que te adora pregunta, Donde estas?*

*Tus ojos son el mismi azul y hermoso cielo,*
*que en mi total ceguera jamas, bien mio, vi;*
*y al descubrirlo siento voraz, febril anhelo*
*de convertime en angel para vivir alli!*

*Quisiera ser un vate de inspiracios ardiente,*
*para pintarte en versos de fuego mi pasion;*
*y con su lumbre luego de intensidad fundente,*
*Fundir dulce bien mio, tu duro corazon.*

*Quisiera a ser posible tener un solo dia*
*la omnipotencia misma, la voluntad de Dios,*
*para tenerte en brazos y asi llamarte mia,*
*Mientras construyo un mundo donde vivir los dos?*

Toñing topped the 1933 board examinations for ship's masters, and now the family had two Captain Basas, father and son. They celebrated with a big party. He had done very well in the 1912 board exams himself, finishing in the top ten, but he had not been Numero Uno. Now his son had outstripped him, and as the father he was very proud of it. That was the fate of a father, to have a son follow in one's footsteps, to be eventually outdone.

The Osmeñas came to Sunday lunch whenever they could. Doña Titay, transplanted from Manila, did not have too many old friends in Cebú and she cherished the company of her old classmate Pilar. As for Don Sergio, he loved Spanish cuisine, and at José M. Basa's table his every whim was indulged. Pilar and her stepdaughter-in-law

Soling did the cooking. Don Sergio had a very punctual appetite, and they always made sure the *comida* was served promptly at 12:00 noon.

Most Filipinos, even Manila Tagalogs, knew only one kind of *adobo*, fried pork chunks, but Pilar and Soling could chose from three Cavíte recipes, and one never knew which to expect. There was the ordinary basic *adobo*, its own oily juices improved with garlic, vinegar and soy sauce; there was *adobo seco*, served with liver sauce; and there was *adobo con caldo* with a red oily sauce.

Whenever they had *kari-kari* its sauce was thickened, in the proper Caviteño way, with *pinipig*, ground toasted rice. Manila people used peanuts—*ique horror!* Pilar learned how her husband liked his *kari-kari*: with a side dish unknown to Manileños, a *kilawin* of radish or green papaya and the internal organs of *lapay* and *librillo*.

Pilar and Soling might cook a *cocido madrileño* with a sauce from eggplant and squash; for this there were side dishes of *nogada* (cabbage) and *potaje de garbanzos* (chickpeas). It was always a meal to be eaten in *aliñar* style.

They might prepare *bacalao a la vizcaina*, or *carne asada* with onion rings, or *callos*, or *tamales*, or *paella*. There were many kinds of paella, but in their family they liked *arroz valenciana* best. They would cook it in a huge flatbottomed round skillet which had two handles and four legs, a *paellera*. Paella never tasted right unless it was eaten from the skillet in which it had been cooked. When they had the Osmeñas over they would serve the paella, in its paellera, on the table. When it was just the family, they would eat alfresco and bring the skillet to the lawn. The whole family would sit on the grass around two paelleras. José M. Basa would take a knife and divide each paella into wedges, like a pie, but leave everything on the paellera;

the wedges were merely to indicate the boundaries of the shares. They would start eating at the edge, work their way inside, and eventually meet at the center. It was as good as a picnic.

José M. Basa was fond of recalling the delightful little surprises Don Sergio found at the Basa table. Once, the Senator was about to taste his *sopa de ajo*, which been topped with bits of softened bread, when Soling stopped him.

*"Un momento, Señor."*

She broke a raw egg over the soup.

"Ah, yes, I had forgotten about that," Osmeña laughed. "So many people serve garlic soup without the egg nowadays."

Another time the main dish was goat meat stew, its rich tomato-based sauce thick with vegetables and condiments.

"The *caldereta* is very good," Doña Titay told Soling. "The meat is very tender, and the sauce is superb."

*"Gracias,"* said Soling.

Over coffee, Osmeña said, "The Ilonggos and the Pampanggos also make very good caldereta, but there is nothing like the caldereta of the Caviteños. By the way, it's been said that the Caviteño caldereta is so rich the ingredients for the sauce cost more than the goat. Is that true?"

"Oh that's just something people say," José M. Basa said. "*Hija*, can you tell us how much you spent for this?"

"Well," Soling said, "*chorizo bilbao* costs so much here..."

When she had tallied it up, Osmeña turned out to have been right: the sauce had indeed cost more than the goat.

"What did I tell you?" Don Sergio laughed.

But when Don Sergio became Vice President in 1935, he could no longer come to Cebú as often as he used to. José M. Basa missed his company. Don Sergio had been the logical candidate for President, but Manuel Quezon had outmaneuvered him. Don Sergio could have fought openly for the nomination, but had preferred to step aside in order to forestall a bruising battle which would probably have divided their followers into two contentious factions. Accepting the Vice Presidential nomination was a great blow to his ambitions but never once did Don Sergio say anything ungracious. It was a display of *delicadeza* only a great man was capable of. It was statesmanship of the highest order.

War was in the air. The Spaniards were not waiting for the rest of the world but were already killing each other, divided as they were into Fascists and Reds. The Japanese took Nanking in 1937. The Germans accomplished the Anschluss in 1938. But Britain's Prime Minister, Chamberlain, still spoke of "peace in our time." The French felt secure behind the Maginot Line.

Britain and France went to war when Germany invaded Poland in 1939, a bit of a surprise as they had not complained when Germany annexed Austria and then grabbed the Sudetenland from Czechoslovakia. The way weak nations could be bullied and eaten up by strong ones gave him the final stanza of "Fatal Augurio":

> *Porque un pueblo cual el nuestro dividido,*
> *por una ley fatal sera absorbido*
> *por otro pueblo mas unido y fuerte!*

That poem finished at last, he gathered it up with the others and published a book, *De Mi Pluma*, Manila 1939. The harvest seemed so meager: in 25 years of writing poetry all it added up to was a thin volume.

The year 1940 seemed unreal, life going on as usual while Europe went mad: Franco occupying Madrid, Paris taken and the Vichy government set up, England left standing alone. The Battle of Britain filled him with a dread fascination. War had become modern. War was fought with fighter aëroplanes, Spitfires and Messerschmitts, as well as with submarines.

In 1941 he knew it could come anytime. Japan and the United States would clash in the Pacific, and the Philippines would be embroiled. When after many months war did not come, he entertained hopes of seeing the year end in peace. Quezon and Osmeña were re-elected President and Vice-President respectively. Then Pearl Harbor was bombed in December. The following day Japanese warplanes bombed Clark Field in Pampanga and Nichols Field near Manila. He knew wars were conducted with lightning swiftness now, but the suddenness of it surprised him.

The Christmas of 1941 was gloomy. The year 1942 saw the fall of Singapore and Malaya and then of Bataan. MacArthur escaped to Australia, promising to return. Quezon and Osmeña were evacuated by submarine from Corregidor to Cebú, then by local fishermen's boats to Mindanao, then from the del Monte plantation airstrip by B-17 bombers to Australia, where the *S.S. Coolidge* was waiting to take them to the United States. But where were the forces America had promised? Roosevelt, it became obvious, was going to follow a "Europe first" policy.

He considered himself to have been forcibly retired from the post of Port Captain of Cebú. He would worry about his pension later. Meanwhile, there was a war on...

Toñing had fled Manila when it was declared an open city, leaving his ship there for the Japanese to commandeer. In Cebú the Japanese commandeered everything: his car, Toñing's car, the houses of the rich. He was fortunate that both their houses were not so prominent. At least they still had places to live in. Pilar started a small bakery. It became their chief means of livelihood. Everyone kept a small vegetable plot and raised whatever animals he could: chickens, ducks, a pig, or a goat.

Cheynoweth, the American brigadier general, surrendered Cebú and the Visayas in May 1942. The Japanese moved in and became José M. Basa's neighbors in Cebú City. The Subetai, a unit of the Imperial Army, "enrolled" at the University of San Cárlos on P. del Rosario Street. The Konobutai, another fighting unit, availed themselves of scholarships at the UP-Cebú College on Gorordo Avenue. The Navy men were fellows at the Cebú Trade School near the piers. The Marines, no schoolboys, took the Gotiaco Building, the first building in Cebú with an elevator, on M.C. Briones Street. The Provincial High School on Jones Avenue, later to be renamed the Abellana High School, became the Japanese garrison's motor pool. Across the street, the Kempetai or Military Police matriculated in the Cebú Normal School. The head of the Kempetai was someone named Tsureyama; his chief investigator was Prince Yoshida, said to be Emperor Hirohito's nephew.

In 1943 it became apparent that the Japanese wanted Toñing's services as a pilot. While José M. Basa had sailed all over the world, Toñing had done more time on the interisland routes. Toñing knew the Philippine islands better than he did. Toñing's year at Annapolis also meant much to the enemy. Toñing's classmates there were now Commanders or Captains in the US Navy; his instructors were now Rear Admirals or Vice Admirals.

Age had something to do with it, too. Loath as José M. Basa was to admit it, the Japanese considered him an old man; the Japanese rendered obeisance to their fathers as no other people did; a Japanese man whose father had died would set up a shrine in the house to worship the departed sire; before the father's picture the Japanese son would daily offer a steaming bowl of rice. A Catholic praying to a saint hardly showed more devotion.

Because of his age, then, the Japanese saw him as a sort of father figure and accorded him something of the filial respect they reserved for their own elders. But they wanted Toñing.

Toñing was in the mountains. José M. Basa had bought some land in Maslog, near Danao in the northern half of Cebú Province, and Toñing had gone there with his family. Toñing's youngest brother Francisco had joined them. Toñing was 41 and in his prime. Of Toñing's children Angel was 18, Nenita 16, Tony 13, Tito 11, Aurora 9, Oscar 7, and Lito 5. José M. Basa and Pilar were left all alone on Jones Avenue: his daughters had all married, except his youngest, Remedios, who had gone with her cousin Nieves to stay with Dr. Lugay in Guiuan.

They kept the bakery going. He had nothing better to do than help Pilar. Wheat was getting scarce, and more and more they used cassava flour. They kneaded dough, rolled it, shaped it into loaves. They burned charcoal and put the glowing coals both below and on top of the ovens. They sampled the results, eating a piece from each batch. By now they were resigned to many deprivations: soup without fresh eggs, meals without wine, coffee made from roasted corn. But they simply could not get used to eating bread without butter.

They minded the store. Women whose husbands, brothers, sons, or fathers were in the Resistance came to buy bread, trade stories of the doings of the guerrillas, and to relay reports heard on well-hidden shortwave radios. News dispatches from the BBC in London or from KGEI in San Francisco, California, often gave the lie to stories in the *Visayan Shimbun*.

A man began coming to the house to call on him, a friendly neighbor, nothing more. This man, who gave his name as Juan Almazan, spoke good Spanish. Almazan addressed him as Capitán Basa at first, then presumed intimacy by abandoning the "usted" forms and calling him Don Pepe. Did Don Pepe still write poetry? Had he published? Yes, he replied, *De Mi Pluma*, Manila 1939. And of course his textbook for mariners, *Nautical Notes*, Manila 1935.

José M. Basa's instincts had been aroused, and later he made discreet inquiries. It was just as he suspected. Almazan's morning hours were often spent at the Cebú Normal School, and his evenings at the Banahaw Coffee Shop or at the Imperial Café. The Banahaw was at the corner of P. del Rosario and Junquera Streets, the Imperial a couple of blocks farther away, at the corner of Sikatuna and D. Jakosalem Streets. Tsureyama and Prince Yoshida were regulars at both cafés. Almazan was a Makapili. A quisling. A collaborator. A spy for the Kempetai.

Almazan came to the house every now and then, usually from the direction of the Cebú Normal School, a ten-minute walk down Jones Avenue. Common decency obliged José M. Basa to offer coffee and pastries from the bakery.

He would politely answer the man's idle questions about his poetry, his few paintings and watercolors, his voyages around the world. He kept his answers short and simple. He did not volunteer anything outside of what was asked. Only by his extreme politeness did he suggest that the visitor was not welcome.

Xérès wine was only a distant memory. It had been Chichang's favorite wine, and Neníta's, too. The aroma of that wine seemed to waft into his nostrils one day when Neníta showed up, a surprise, to fetch something she had left in one of the rooms. She would stay with them for a few days, she said. Life in the mountains bored her. She could help Lola Pilar with the baking of the bread.

He realized she could be taken hostage by the Japanese but there was nothing to do: she was there. Neníta's vivacity was infectious; she sparkled with charm and youthfulness, brightening up the whole house. Neníta resembled Chichang very much: the same gypsy eyes, the same glossy, wavy hair, the sense of something wild, something untamed about her. Hadn't she been an infant only yesterday? And here she was, sixteen years old. Her very presence seemed to induce drunkenness. Chichang had been this age, sixteen, when he took her to wife.

Almazan came, had coffee. He made the usual idle chatter. Pilar told Neníta to stay in her room, but Almazan must have sensed her.

Jose M. Basa sent word via the men of the Resistance. He hoped they could arrange to have Neníta brought to safety in the mountains.

Almazan was back the following day, a Japanese officer in tow.

*"Pronto,"* Pilar said, thrusting Neníta into a plaited-bamboo clothes hamper and throwing dirty clothes in after her. *"Quieta."*

"Where is she?"

"She went back to her family," José M. Basa said. The Japanese officer angrily said something in his guttural language.

"I don't believe that," Almazan said. "She's still here."

"Her mother came to get her," Pilar said, talking fast, saying whatever came to mind, "I wanted her here to help me with the kneading of the dough, but..."—hoping talk would distract or convince them.

The officer stormed into the room. He noticed the hamper, saw it was too small for anyone but a child to fit inside. All the same he whipped out his katana, savagely thrust it into the hamper, then just as quickly pulled the weapon out again.

Almazan came back from the bedrooms, said something to the officer.

"Let's go," the Japanese said, or something like that, "we're wasting time."

They left in a huff.

Pilar opened the hamper.

Miraculously, Neníta was unhurt.

"I felt it sliding past me," she said as her grandparents hugged her, "it was only an inch away..."

A woman buying bread at the bakery told them Soling had arrived that afternoon, on horseback, leading a spare mount. She was waiting for them. As soon as it was dark, José M. Basa brought Neníta to the rendezvous. There was time only for hurried goodbyes. Soling and Neníta mounted the horses and galloped off.

"I have men waiting," one of the voices in the dark assured José M. Basa. "As soon as they've crossed the bridge, my men will blow it up. Should make it that much harder to follow them."

"Yankee doodle came to town..." hummed a Resistance leader's wife. A silly tune, but she had heard it on shortwave radio. It was January 1944, and the tide was turning. He had heard about the Battle of Midway, and he understood better than most what the American victory there meant. The Americans would come in force soon, as MacArthur had promised. The war would be won. But the enemy would not give up easily.

They were up in the mountains now, he and Pilar, out of the crossfire. There would soon be street-by-street fighting in Cebú.

He knew the Americans would come in from the Pacific, and land in Mindanao first. Or perhaps Samar, or Lingayen.

He knew Almazan would track Toñing down eventually, and lead a platoon of Japanese to Maslog. Everything was drifting farther away from him. He was no longer in the thick of things. But he could watch from the sidelines, almost as though he had been granted the gift of second sight.

He seemed to see them: Toñing, and Mary Renner-Osmeña, who was German-American, and Mary's mother Eulalia Renner, and Mary's children, Sonny, Lito, and Annie, aged 7, 5, and 3. The Americans had landed in Leyte. They had brought the President-in-exile along with them: he could see Don Sergio, in a nondescript khaki uniform, wading ashore beside General MacArthur, the latter with his sunglasses and his corncob pipe, and the four stars gleaming golden on his collar. The Americans were in radio contact with the Resistance in Cebú, and would be sending a PT boat from Guiuan to a beach near Maslog to pick up the Osmeñas. Capt. Basa would be taken along, too.

Don Sergio's grandchildren were much like his own: he had grandchildren who were the same age. He pitied the Osmeña kids. Their father, Dr. Emilio Osmeña, a Lieutenant Colonel in the USAFFE, had been executed by the Japanese. He grieved for Don Sergio, who had lost three sons in this war: Peping and Doring, José Osmeña and Teodoro Osmeña, had also been killed. Don Sergio was indeed President now, having succeeded Quezon upon the latter's sudden death in América, but he was also just another bereft father.

Toñing would get away, and the Osmeñas, but that would leave Soling and her children in the lurch. They too would have to find a way to reach Guiuan. The east coast of Cebú would no longer be safe. He knew Soling would see that. The west coast would be the only way. He could imagine them: Soling and her seven children, the youngest only 5, and his own youngest son, Francisco, and perhaps a local farmer or two to guide them, making the difficult trek across the backbone of Cebú from Maslog to Tuburan. Somehow he knew one of the locals, a yokel of 20, was enamored of Neníta. This ardent young swain would carry a guitar across the mountains, biding his time, hoping she would notice him, waiting for the opportunity to serenade her. Very picaresque, but that was how he saw it.

Zarzuelas continued to be staged; the Japanese made the motions of promoting local culture. He and Pilar had gone to see one, and from there had made good their escape. The false gaiety of the zarzuela stayed with him.

"He kept cracking silly jokes from the zarzuela," Joe Basa told me. "He nearly got Lola Pilar's goat."

Joe was drunk now, and so was I. When I was drunk, I got lazy and apathetic. Joe, I knew, would get very maudlin.

"Death came for him like a thief in the night," Joe said. "They had gone to some mountain village where Lola Pilar knew a few people, old people who had fought with her uncle in the Tres de Abril revolt. They had been given a room in some hut. Lola Pilar had gone to the outhouse. Lolo Pepe was standing up, doing something, when he got the heart attack. She found him dead on the floor."

"How did she know it was a heart attack?"

"Oh, Dr. Lugay had warned him. Rich diet, cigars, and all that..."

"That was 1944. For three years they'd been doing without rich food. You said he missed butter."

"Nenita's brush with that sword had something to do with it. He must have sensed that the family's escape would be just as close. He worried about Almazan tracking down Tio Toñing."

"Did he?"

"Yes. Almazan was a zealot in a way. He considered it his mission in life to personally hand over the renowned pilot to Admiral Kurita or Admiral Nishimura, whichever of them would make a stop in Cebu. One wishes Lolo Pepe had known how things turned out. But Lolo died before he could know. It was not his fate to know. He was not to know about the PT boat that picked up Tio Toñing and the Osmeñas. He was not to know about Tia Soling leading her whole family on foot across the mountains all the way to Tuburan. He was not to know about the banca Tia Soling chartered in Tuburan, for 500 pesos. None of it in Mickey Mouse money. It was all Commonwealth-issue money. The banca took a week to reach Calicoan Island near Guiuan, sailing only by night. Too bad Lolo Pepe didn't live long enough to know how things turned out."

But I was not so sure of that. Would he not have experienced, in the last fleeting instants of his earthly life, what the French call *presque vu*? In the throes of his heart attack, between the moment the pain became unbearable and the moment he fell to the ground, would not his whole life have passed before his eyes? Wouldn't the gift of second sight have shown him his family's outcome too, and their deliverance? I somehow thought it might have been like that.

I knew what he would have seen: Toñing and the Osmeñas escaping in the nick of time, and the Japanese patrol led by Almazan arriving at the beach and firing their machine guns at the receding PT boat.

But in his vision of it the machine guns were going *Pac-bung!* like a squad of Remingtons, the bullets were not describing straight lines but arcs, and helplessly he watched as they curved through time and space, and hit him in the back.

At the last moment, he understood he must fall supine and be found lying face up. He managed to wrench around and spin on his heel, an incredible effort.

He was dead before he hit the ground.

# afterword

"Enosis" uses the Greek word ενοσισ in its original sense. While *enosis* has for some time been a one-word slogan for ethnic Greeks on Cyprus who advocate union with the Hellenic Republic of Greece, no such political connotations are implied in the story.

"Vietnik" is based on a true story. Old Mandaue hands tell different versions of it, but they all agree on the aircraft types involved: a B-52 on the way out, a C-130 on the way back.

"Close to the Bone" is based entirely on research.

"Du-awon" describes a place unique to the eighties. In the nineties many of its chasms were filled in, the northernmost cove was lost to an adjoining hotel's golf course, and my favorite ladder allowed to rust away. In September 1995 the Codilla family sold Du-awon to FILINVEST Land Inc.

"Glossolalia" should be read aloud by three readers, one after another at first, then all three together in metrically identical cacophony. The result should prove worthy of the Miriam Defensor Santiago Dictionary's definition of "glossolalia".

The speakers in "Glossolalia" are a Neolithic man at Stonehenge; Sri Lumay Bataugong, the legendary founder of Sugbu (Cebu); and Gringo Honasan's pet python, in that order.